CW01560561

Acknowledg

I would like to thank Katielynn Parrott Johnson for both her fabulous artwork and her help in editing this book.

I would also like to thank T J for her help with editing and her creative suggestions.

CHAPTER ONE

-Before It All-

At first, Marcus barely noticed it. He had thought to himself, that it was just something unusual in the rearview mirror. He had noticed an odd feature in the sky. Given his past, and what he had been through, he was reluctant to look back again. Surely, Marcus thought to himself, this could not have any possible connection to where he was now.

Ed was driving, and talking about the future. The surrounding area was a flat and basically featureless desert. It had looked like this for hundreds of miles, in the burning heat. Nothing really, only a few struggling strands of vegetation wound their scrawny limbs towards the sky. The plants were determined survivors, thought Marcus. After what he had been through just recently, he could relate to that.

His exit from L.A. had been quick and organized, just as he had planned. Hardly anyone had seen him leaving, except the kind old lady who fed him banana pudding. He was glad he had managed to have an opportunity to say goodbye to her earlier. Even though they had never spoken about it, she had known, and she had tried to help him. Once he had loaded all of his possessions into Ed's van, he had felt good. But, it was not until they finally drove over the state line, heading away from California, that he felt he could relax a little.

"I think we should find a motel soon, I am getting pretty tired," said Ed. "Of course, whatever you need," replied Marcus. "I need a beer and then a good night's sleep, that's what I need. My back is aching, and we have a lot of Texas to cover tomorrow." said Ed.

Suddenly, Ed stopped himself. "Hey, do you see that cloud up there? Look behind you? It's really weird."

"Is it the white one, with what looks like a golden middle to it? Yeah, I saw it," replied Marcus. "It was way behind us when I first saw it. You must have good eyes if you can see it at this range."

"It is Not way behind us now," said Ed, "it looks like it is coming right at us! That is freaking me out! Turn around man, and see for yourself!"

Marcus recognized the urgency in Ed's voice, and snapped his head around immediately. Not only did the cloud appear to be gaining on them, its `core ` or middle, now radiated a golden glow, while the rest of it had changed from white to pink.

"What speed are you doing?" said Marcus.

"About sixty miles an hour," replied Ed.

"Then how can it be possibly gaining on us?" Marcus said. Now, he was turned around and was transfixed by it.

"I have no idea at all," said Ed, in a slow and careful manner. "It's one of the strangest things I have ever seen in my whole life. I keep thinking it must be some kind of misperception, due to us travelling in a moving vehicle. You can see it too, and there is no doubt at all that it is moving nearer and nearer."

"I can't deny that", said Marcus. "It's pretty damn strange."

"What do you think it could be?" said Ed.

"I can't associate it with any weather phenomenon that I am aware of," said Marcus, sounding puzzled. "Really, I have no idea at all what it could be."

"We are only a few miles from that little town we were planning on stopping in," said Ed, "I would like to pull over and take a photograph of it, and see what it does."

"By all means go for it," said Marcus, "take a photo, but I can tell you that there is something malevolent about it."

Ed turned to Marcus, who could see that he was worried. Then he said, "you mean like before? Not like the others, surely? I can't see the connection, but I totally trust your instincts."

"No, not like them fortunately, it is a different energy. But, I don't think it's good. That is all I can tell you right now," said Marcus.

"I understand, "said Ed. "I vote we stop the car, get a quick photo of it, and then shoot straight for the town."

"Agreed" replied Marcus.

Ed pulled the car over into the dirt, by the side of the road. It was getting dark, and in front of them the lights of the town beamed in the distance.

As Ed stood up to get out of the car, Marcus stopped him. "I think we should keep the engine running," said Marcus, "just in case."

Ed nodded in agreement, "sure thing," he said, and switched it back on.

Marcus stepped out of the car, and saw the cloud rushing towards them.

"As soon as we stopped, that thing actually increased speed!" He shouted towards Ed. "It's like it is coming to intercept us!"

"You are right, "said Ed. "What the hell is it, and what does it want?"

"I have no idea what it is, but I feel like what it wants is going to be seriously bad for us!" exclaimed Marcus.

"I agree!" said Ed, "Let's get out of here!"

It was then that the cloud attacked. Marcus watched aghast, as it seemed to vibrate and shoot out a bolt straight towards Ed, just as he was taking a video of it. Ed jumped back in response.

Marcus clearly heard a popping sound, as the lightning that emanated from it, hit the ground. This was followed by a thin plume of smoke.

Marcus and Ed gave each other the briefest of glances, before they both shot back into the car. Ed stepped on the accelerator, and the van screamed in protest, as they skidded off towards the town.

The cloud instantly responded to this, and it also picked up speed. It began hurtling towards the car, again vibrating as it did so. The cloud launched another bolt towards the van, which exploded behind its bumper.

The van now lurched from sixty to ninety, in just a few seconds, as the town sign became visible. It was now only a few hundred feet in front of them.

Ed's teeth were gritted as he rasped, "I don't think we are going to get away from it! The acceleration on that thing is incredible!"

"Just keep going!"said Marcus. "I can't tell you why, but I think it will stop when we get to the town."

Ed kept looking straight ahead but nodded his compliance. "I need you to be right, or we are a barbecue." With that, he squeezed the last bit of acceleration out of the van, and it flew into the town. The streets had been deserted, but now they could see cars just a few hundred yards in front of them, cruising the town's main strip.

Marcus glanced back at the cloud. It suddenly did a sharp turn at the town's main welcome sign, before shooting up into the sky and disappearing into the black, bald, desert sky.

"You were right," shouted Ed triumphantly, "The bastard's gone!"

"Yes," replied Marcus, the relief in his voice palpable.

"But how did you know?"

"I can't tell you," said Marcus. "But I can tell you this."

"What is it?" asked Ed, interrupting.

"Rarely have a wanted a drink more in my life!" Marcus exclaimed.

Ed chuckled in response. Then he said, "Let's do it!"

The next morning, Marcus struggled to open his eyes. It felt like they had been sewn shut. Furious blinking, he eventually got them working. He and Ed grabbed some coffee, before setting off on the road. Ed added his usual, thirteen spoonfuls of sugar into his coffee.

"I rarely drink or do drugs, and this is my morning high", said Ed, stirring it furiously as he spoke. Then he added, "I am hoping today will be uneventful. I think we can get most of the way through Texas, before we rest. Given the events of last night though, I am going to stop when it gets dark, and make sure we are in a population center when we do so."

"I agree," said Marcus. "I don't sense that the cloud, or whatever it was, is following us, but we are not in too much of a hurry."

"That's right," said Ed. "I have to transport my pet cargo after I drop you off. But, I don't have to be in Tennessee for at least four days, so I have plenty of time to do that. I was actually thinking of stopping off at the Bonnie and Clyde Museum in Louisiana on the way to Ohio. I know you are keen to see her, but do you have time to do that?"

"Yes, I am really keen to see her. After all I have been through, it's the start of a new life together," Marcus replied. "The Museum would be a good stop however, if it isn't too far out of the way."

"It won't mean more than a few hours difference to the journey," Ed replied.

"Let's do it then," said Marcus.

The morning journey through Texas was uneventful. The scenery felt pretty much like Arizona. For hundreds of miles, there had been nothing but hot and dry scrubland.

That night, they rested in a town, the name of which Marcus didn't bother to absorb. He was busy thinking of her now. He hadn't seen Aubrey in months. Of course, he missed her. She had an amazing smile, beautiful auburn hair and a toned, athletic physique. There was also no doubt about it, she was very smart indeed. They had first become friends after meeting at a conference three years ago. He had been entranced with her, ever since.

During his last visit, in March, she had asked him to come and move in with her and her two youngest children. Her son Seth was fourteen, and her daughter Betsy was eighteen. Her eldest, Landon, who was twenty, lived on his own nearby.

She said that she would get everything ready so he could be ready by to move in by the 22 nd of June. He and Ed had planned his move from California to Ohio around arriving on that very date.

There was no doubt that it was a big step for all of them, but Marcus felt he was ready.

The following morning, the desert gradually began to transform into woodland. Marcus had nothing against the desert. In fact, he had spent many enjoyable days and nights in the California deserts, most notably the Anza Borrego. To him, they had had a stark beauty all of their own. What the changing of the scenery meant to Marcus though, was that he was getting nearer to Aubrey.

At first, he wasn't sure that he had seen it. It was moving fast, and it was only a shape after all, so he dismissed it. Then he saw it again, ten miles later.

The same shape. Weirdly, the shape of it looked almost like a man, he thought. It seemed like it was keeping pace with the car. It would appear for a few seconds, then completely disappear.

"Given that we saw that strange cloud, I thought I should tell you that I have seen some strange shapes and movements in the woods a few times since we started to see trees," said Marcus to Ed.

"What do you mean strange shapes?" said Ed, frowning as he turned to Marcus.

"Well, they almost seemed man like, for want of a better description. They are moving very quickly, like they were trying to keep pace with us."

"Was it big?" said Ed.

"It's difficult for me to judge," Marcus replied, "looking through a moving vehicle and all, but I would say yes it was. I would have dismissed them if I had just seen them once, but I have seen it or them a few times now. I thought you should know."

"What do you think it was?" said Ed. "After all these years of looking, do you actually think you might have caught a glimpse of a Bigfoot?"

"No, I am not saying that," said Marcus. "I can't be sure of what I saw. I just felt like something was, 'off '. Something was not right."

Ed nodded in response. "Well, I know you can feel certain things. Let me know if you see anything like that again. I am going to stick to the freeway anyway, until we get to Alabama. We can find somewhere there to rest tonight."

As darkness approached, they headed into Alabama, and began looking for a motel to spend the night. Ed was getting pretty tired, and the day's traveling had gone to plan.

It was difficult to find anywhere to stay, but eventually they found a less than salubrious basic motel, only five miles off of the freeway. It offered a couple of beds and looked reasonably clean.

There were only a few residents of the motel, but nonetheless, Marcus was glad that they were given a room well out of the way of the other people in the place. They were assigned a room in the far corner of the motel. Understandably, after a day of hard driving, Ed pretty much crashed as soon as he got in and started snoring almost straight away.

Marcus on the other hand, mostly stayed awake, excitedly thinking about his new life with Aubrey.

The lights had not been out for more than a couple of minutes before they heard it. It was a scurrying sound, followed by a chattering noise.

Ed immediately shot up in his bed. "What the hell is that?" He said. "Did you hear it?"

"Yes, I did," said Marcus. Reaching for his bedside light. Standing there, in the middle of the room, was a giant cockroach. It had not scurried away when the light was turned on, as these creatures were akin to do, rather it seemed almost defiant.

Ed threw his shoe at the creature, which dodged it and then resumed its position, "I missed the fucking thing," said Ed.

Marcus slipped out of his bed, and keeping his eye on the creature, put on his boots carefully and slowly. Then, in a fluid movement, he hurled himself across the room and brought his foot down hard on the floor. The creature however, had managed to dodge him, and now it turned.

"It's heading towards you!" Shouted Ed, throwing his other shoe as he did so. The shoe made the creature swerve, and this time Marcus did not miss it. His boot crunched through shell, and then soft goo. Only a few writhing legs remained amidst the splatter.

"That was the biggest damn cockroach I have ever seen!" exclaimed Ed.

"Yes, but that was no ordinary cockroach," said Marcus. "You saw what it did. It didn't scurry away like normal cockroaches do, and it also turned and seemingly attacked me!"

"Yes," I would agree. As strange as it sounds, and we have seen some very strange things, brother," said Ed. "It really did look like it was after you."

The following morning, they drove towards the Museum. The Louisiana air was thick and humid, but Marcus still enjoyed it. It was very different from low humidity he was used to in L.A.

Bonnie Parker was petite and pretty, standing just four feet eleven inches tall. She also seemed never to have fired a gun, unlike Clyde, who could have killed up to ten people. They, and their gang, mostly participated in small scale robbery. They both led short violent lives and had become international icons.

The public was so fascinated. Just moments after they drew their lasts breaths, crowds had gathered at the scene, to steal 'souvenirs'. The crowds 'ripped' items off the car they were shot in, and even off of the bodies themselves. These human vultures would probably not see any moral discrepancy in their actions, Marcus mused to himself, as he walked around the museum. It was fascinating to see what ends up making people famous.

Bonnie craved fame. She apparently had been kind to others, had a good sense of humor, and she was smart by all accounts. Bonnie had a gift at writing poetry. Bonnie had some positive attributes, but she had chosen to hook up with violent and murderous men. Her husband and Clyde, were both nasty men. She had achieved fame, but she had to pay a high price for it.

The place where Bonnie and Clyde had met their end, was not far from the Museum. Ed was keen to go visit the site. On arrival, Marcus got out of the car, and headed towards the memorial stone. Then, something to his right, caught his eye. In the woods behind the monument, he saw something black and fleeting. The dark shape shot past him at a very high speed. It looked like the shadow of a huge man. They had seen similar shadows, moving in the same way, in Texas.

"Ed, it is here. Whatever it is." said Marcus.

Ed stopped, nodded and then began to walk towards him very slowly.

"Did you see it? Get a good look at it?" asked Ed.

"No, it was something fleeting, just like before." Marcus replied.

"Any sense, any feeling?" asked Ed.

"No, nothing like that at all." said Marcus.

"Good." said Ed.

They both stood in silence, listening for a minute, but there was nothing to hear but birdsong. After that they walked into the tree line, both carefully inspecting for prints. But, whatever had shot past Marcus, had left no evidence of itself at all.

It was the following day that they crossed from Kentucky into Ohio. Marcus's heart jumped, as he knew he was now only a few hours drive from Adams County, where Aubrey lived.

"Marcus, I just want to say one thing to you about Aubrey. I wasn't going to mention it. But, considering the events of the past few days, I must," said Ed.

"What is it?" Asked Marcus.

"I know that Aubrey is fascinated by the paranormal, and everything associated with it," said Ed.

"Yes," said Marcus.

"There is an old saying," said Ed, "If you look at evil, then It looks back at you. I know you have heard this phrase before, but maybe it applies to paranormal things too. You don't know much about what she is really into."

"I understand what you mean," said Marcus, "but I think things will be totally fine. I am not worried about the paranormal stuff. I'm more concerned about fitting in with the family."

"Okay, okay, " said Ed. "Listen though, if you ever do have problems, please call me, even if it is in the middle of the night, and I will come and get you, okay?"

"I promise", replied Marcus.

"Do you mean it?" Said Ed.

"Absolutely", replied Marcus, "I give you my word."

CHAPTER TWO

-The Beginning-

Rural Ohio was now his home, thought Marcus, as he and Ed passed through green rolling farmland. There were scattered small towns, made up of mostly plain, white houses.

Adams County, which was Ohio's most rural county, was where Aubrey's family had lived for generations. Her home, nestled in the foothills of the Appalachian Mountain range, had been owned by them for generations. Marcus had visited it three times before this last trip, and now it was to be his home too.

Aubrey had told him that there was a long history of super natural incidents at her home. For example, she described the ghost of a young girl, who she said regularly liked to play on the stairs. She was very convinced, that a 'old man' spirit, was her 'very own personal spirit'.

Very intriguingly, she also said that there was some kind of portal, around the front door. The portal worked, or to use her own words, 'pulsed intermittently.' It had the ability to `move time`, she had said, and that her and her children often felt nauseous around it.

On his visits there, Marcus had experienced no activity from any of these spirits or phenomenon. Aubrey had assured him that it was just a matter of time before he did. She had also told him to keep that to himself, "as the spirits might not like it if he talked about them."

He hadn't been too concerned about this before, but the events of the last few days had left him disturbed, and as day fell to night, he decided to confide in Ed and tell him all about them.

"Man, that would certainly raise some serious red flags for most guys," said Ed.

Then he added, "and I don't want to sound rude, but I would run a mile if some woman said that to me."

"I understand," said Marcus, "and I want you to know that I did think carefully about it. In a way though, it kind of excites me if that makes sense."

Ed laughs at this and then said, "I thought you might have learned your lesson after Oregon, but I guess not. Last chance to turn around now though, we are only thirty minutes away. You can come and stay with me and Jessica for as long as you want, at least until you figure out what to do next."

"You know I am not going to do that," said Marcus. "I am committed now. I am all in. I am excited to begin my new life."

"I know we have joked about it," said Ed, his tone serious, "but I would figure out a plan B if I were you. I will always be there for you, but it's worth it."

"I understand," said Marcus. "I did speak to Johnny about it, the guy who runs one of the main conferences here, you remember him?"

"Yes," said Ed, "the guy who organized the conference you spoke at in May? I met him once, he seems a nice guy."

"Yeah, that's the one," said Marcus. Then he added, "he lives in northern Ohio, about three hours away, probably too far in an emergency. He does have a friend however, Dusty, who is only thirty minutes down the road. I was going to contact this guy anyway, as he has done a lot of bigfoot research in the area."

"I would like to see if he would be prepared to share information with me, and to advise me on local hotspots. He may prove a useful resource in more ways than one, if need be." said Marcus.

"That's good, said Ed, "I am glad you at least have that."   Ed now took the car into a swerve up a small country lane. The road was steep, heading up a heavily forested mountainside. "Could this place be any more remote?" He said, "anyway, we will be there in a few minutes."

"Great!" Replied Marcus. "I will call Aubrey. She wanted to arrange it, so that she and her kids would be outside waiting for us."

As they approached the crooked white house that was to be his new home, Marcus could see Aubrey waiting in the driveway. She had her hands on her hips as normal. This would normally be seen as a sign of irritation or defiance in most people, but Marcus knew Aubrey enough now to understand that this was just a normal posture for her.

He had discussed with her several times about how she should have been a dancer. Indeed, she moved with a certain liquidity. When she walked, she almost seemed to glide, so light was she on her feet. He had joked that she was in fact an elf, and she tried to play up to it, and did a handstand and finished with a twirl.

Aubrey ran up to him just as he was getting out of the car and showered him with tiny kisses. She gripped him tightly, which caused Marcus to wince slightly, as he remembered how strong she was.

"Oh, thank goodness you are here!" said Aubrey. "Finally! After all this time! You must be exhausted! Seth, Betsy! Come and say hello to Marcus and Ed."

"Hi, nice to see you again," said Betsy, who also sported the same long auburn hair as her mother. She also had the same angular face and eyes as Aubrey and was unmistakably like her.

Considering he was only thirteen, what first struck Ed was how tall Seth seemed for his age. He looked nothing like Aubrey or Betsy. He was stout and very broad shouldered, with a long shock of red hair. Unlike Aubrey and Betsy, who were quite dark skinned, Seth's skin was pale, almost translucent. Seth politely offered Marcus and Ed water, before he began taking boxes out of the van.

As he began unpacking the van , Ed started to feel uncomfortable around Seth. There was just something about him, and Ed wasn't sure what it was, that just seemed off. Seth had a quiet intensity about him, but there was more to it than that though. There was certainly nothing substantial enough for him to worry Marcus about. Marcus just seemed so happy, thought Ed. And boy, his friend had certainly had things tough. He just really hoped it all worked out well for him here.

With the unpacking done, it was time for Ed to say his goodbye's. "Well, good luck buddy," said Ed, as he drew deep on the cigarette he was puffing." I hope everything works out, and as I said, if you need me, please call. I hope I see you soon."

"Thanks Ed," said a visibly happy Marcus.

Ed watched as they all entered the house, First Betsy, then Seth, followed by Marcus and Aubrey, the latter with her arm wrapped tight around Marcus's waist.

Ed got in his car and reset his phone's G.P.S. It was six hours to his home in Tennessee. He planned to have a break on the way, and then crash as soon as he got home. He had a lot of hauling to do straight after that, all the way back to Los Angeles with plenty of stops along the way, and he needed a couple of days rest before he did that.

Driving off, he looked out of the rearview mirror as he left. Something standing there watching him in the back upstairs window, a figure, maybe a girl? He couldn't tell for sure, as he only got a quick look at whatever it was. Should he call Marcus and tell him? Not on the basis of a quick glimpse, Ed decided, and anyway what would Marcus say? It was just one of the ghosts, nothing to worry about. He resolved to call his friend within the next few days if he didn't hear from him.

Marcus sat down, and as he did so, he immediately felt a wave of exhaustion pass over him.

"Ah babe, you look exhausted," said Aubrey, "Here, have this. I have made you one of my special teas to help you sleep. Drink it, and then let's go to bed. We can start on your unpacking in the morning."

"Thanks so much, my love, I will," said Marcus in response.

Aubrey sent Betsy and Seth to their rooms upstairs, while she and Marcus retired to what was now their bedroom downstairs. Aubrey fell asleep almost instantly, and Marcus listened to her breathing lightly next to him for a few minutes. When she turned away from him, she rolled with the blanket, leaving him without it. The start of things to come, Marcus chuckled to himself.

Then, to his astonishment, as he lay there, the blanket then lifted itself up and began wrapping around him, holding him tight, almost as if he were a swaddling baby! Aubrey hadn't moved. Something, or someone else had done it, there was no doubt about that! It was amazing, but Marcus decided not to investigate, there was plenty of time for that in the future. He needed to pace himself, and he felt he wasn't in danger if all the entity was going to do was to wrap him up.

He let sleep take him. There was plenty to do tomorrow, and he was going to need all his energy, it seemed. Besides, his body felt so leaden, he wasn't even sure he could open is eyes even if he wanted to.

Marcus normally jumped straight out of bed, but the next morning he felt groggy. He was an early riser by nature, while Aubrey was mostly nocturnal. Marcus was a teacher by trade and was going to continue this by working from home part time, for four hours a day. Given that there was a three-hour time difference between the west and east coast, all his classes would be in the afternoon, which gave him time, he hoped to adjust to Aubrey's schedule a bit. It wouldn't do well for the relationship if he was barely able to keep his eyes open at 11p.m. while she was wide awake, and didn't go to sleep until 3am.

At first, he sat in her living room and waited, unsure what to do. The room was littered with coke cans, sneakers, and other teenage stuff. He wasn't a neat freak he thought to himself, he could cope with this.

He decided to wander into the kitchen and grab himself a cereal bar and some coffee. Aubrey had suggested he help himself to anything in the kitchen if he felt like it, as she had anticipated that he might be up well before her.

After downing some cold coffee, he decided to head out into the garden and explore a bit. The old white house was unusual in itself, he considered. It looked older, much older than many of the wooden timber houses he had seen on the way up here. It also leaned a little to one side, but in a strange, twisted way. It was almost as if the house was resisting the earth, which was trying to suck it up.

The grounds were large, almost three acres Marcus guessed. There were a few huts contained within it, a large fire pit, and a majestic looking maple tree. The tree stood at the bottom of the property, almost parallel to the house. About halfway across the acreage, was a chicken coop. Marcus counted seven plump chickens and a rooster in it. He could also see nesting boxes. Aubrey had said that if there was one thing they would never be short of, it was eggs.

The fire pit intrigued him. It was especially large he considered, with huge, blackened stones around bordering its circumference. It was also well used he observed, even recently, as the grass around it was well flattened and the ground trampled as though many people had been here. Marcus did not recall Aubrey saying she had had any social events recently. He would have to ask her about it.

After being cramped in the car all day, he decided to stretch his legs and walk around the periphery of the property and take stock of the woodland and farmland beyond. The air here was so clean he thought, much better than the L.A. smog. He had a lot of adjusting to do, but he would get used to it. Then, his thoughts on this subject stopped dead, as he turned to see the strange markings in the ground.

Three long straight lines, about three feet across, had been carved into the ground. Marcus could see that the markings were deep. Underneath them were what could only be described as strange waves, followed by a small circle. It was at a direct right angle to the house. What was the significance of this drawing, Marcus wondered? He began striding towards the extreme left-hand side of the house. He walked past the fire pit. He paused and noticed that there seemed to be another drawing in the fire pit. This one was obscured, to some extent, by charcoal and partially burnt wood. He reasoned that this explained why he did not see it the first time.

Then, he was startled when he heard "Hi babe!" directly behind him. It was Aubrey. She had always managed to sneak up on him, throughout their relationship. Indeed, Aubrey had an almost incredible ability to suddenly appear right by his side, and she delighted in it. She laughed as she said it. She had a deep, throaty laugh.

"Good morning!" said Marcus in response. "I thought you might not be up for a while, so I decided to go on a little walk to check out your property."

"Of course, my love," replied Aubrey "I was up earlier too, and I was excited that you are here. It is our property now. This is your home too."

"Yes, yes, it is," replied Marcus smiling. He went to hug Aubrey, and felt her chin press against his shoulder as she gave him a squeeze back.

"Would you like to get some breakfast in town? We could pick up some ham and egg muffins maybe? And I know an excellent coffee place. Does that sound good? Maybe I could also give you a little tour of Ollenberry, if you'd like?" said Aubrey.

"That sounds perfect," said Marcus. Then he asked, "can you tell me what these strange symbols are, on the ground here. I found one over there, and it looks like there is one in the fire pit. I have never seen anything like them before."

"Why yes of course, Aubrey replied. They are called sigils. They are protection symbols, magical symbols. I could give a long answer, but basically, they ward things off, or cause things to appear, depending on what you draw of course. We have our own family symbols. The one you see in the fire pit,is a protection one."

"It looks like you had quite a few people here when you drew this one", said Marcus. "The ground around it is all flattened." Marcus saw just a flitter of irritation pass across Aubrey's face, before she buried it.

"No, just me and the kids. We had a barbecue here a couple of weeks ago, and it hasn't rained since then. In fact, we were planning on having one tonight to celebrate you being here. Betsy's friend Trina was going to come over, and my Uncle John if you are okay with that? We might as well get some provisions for it while we are in town."

"That sounds good," said Marcus," let's do that."

Aubrey's house was located around ten miles from the town. There were no sidewalks or even dirt tracks between the town and her house, just a collection of farms. They varied between arable and livestock. As they were driving along, Marcus recognized the tall stalks growing in the fields. He had never seen corn fields before. Los Angeles was not exactly known for them.

"I have seen it so many times in movies, I would love to run though a cornfield here"

Aubrey laughed in response. "Well, that can be arranged, but you are going to have to be careful because them farmers would set their dogs on you or worse, if they catch you in those fields of theirs," she said.

"What could be worse than being set upon by a pack of dogs?" said Marcus.

Aubrey replied "We will find you a quiet place to run, babe, no worries."

Ollenberry looked like something from a bygone era, thought Marcus. Almost like a painting, or one of those historic black and white photographs. The main strip was composed of wooden and brick built Victorian buildings, across four main streets. In the center was a courthouse and a town hall. There were also curious little shops. A jewelry shop for example, what looked like a bookshop, and an old-fashioned sweet shop.

"I remember seeing one of those when I was a kid," said Marcus, I would love to go in there, and the bookshop sometime, if that's okay?" Marcus said to Aubrey.

"Of course," she replied, "I thought you might, with your sweet tooth."

"When I was a child, my granny used to take me to one run by an old lady called Marion, who was lovely. She had big jars of sweets stretching up to the ceiling. I used to choose some from the jars, and Marion would put them in a little paper bag. I remember how excited I was to get my little bag. I would cling onto it all the way back to my granny's house." said Marcus.

Evil In Ollenberry

After the town hall, and the central old-fashioned strip, there were more modern shops. "The town elders wanted to keep the historical integrity of the town intact," explained Aubrey. "So, no chain stores in the center."

"I support that," said Marcus "I prefer a town with character when you wander through it. That makes it feel like the town is speaking to you from the past. It's depressing to see every town look the same."

Aubrey flashed him a smile. "I am so glad. The only old-fashioned shop that sits outside this area is Tate's. It's a hardware store. Tate's was originally built on a hill just outside of town. It was built hundreds of years ago. Nobody is exactly sure when. I don't think. The Tate family still owns it. I know you are not exactly a DIY enthusiast, but it's interesting to wander around, and you could also see if they are hiring, once you settle in a bit."

"Good idea," said Marcus. "I certainly want to check the place out."

The shops outside of the town were the same generic one's, and so it was easy for Marcus to pick out what they needed for the barbecue. Once they had loaded up with what they needed, they headed off to the coffee place that Aubrey had been so enthusiastic about.

It was a few miles outside of town, down a small winding lane. The coffee shop was unremarkable. In fact, it looked weather beaten and gnarled. Marcus noticed that it leaned towards the ground, in the same way that Aubrey's house did.

"This is quite an out of the way place to locate a coffee shop," said Marcus.

"This used to be an old trading route," Aubrey explained. "It was once the main route into town. The locals know where it is though, and they come. The locals always come to support our businesses. Though I am sure they get the occasional lucky guest."

"I guess I am a lucky guest today," said Marcus.

"No babe, you are much more than that, you live here now, you are a local, or at least you will be when people get used to you."

They pulled into the coffee shop, and the window to the hut was immediately drawn back by a man with long scraggly hair. He was thin, with circular glasses, which he peered over as he smiled at Aubrey.

"How are you, Pete?" Said Aubrey.

"I am real good, real good," replied Pete.

"And how is Jenny?"

"She's good too," said Pete. Marcus was aware that Pete was staring at him, so he returned his gaze and smiled.

"Well, who do we have here?" said Pete, addressing Aubrey. "Is this the guy we have been waiting for? Your fiancée? He finally showed up, did he? Me and Jenny were beginning to wonder."

"Jenny is Pete's sister," said Aubrey to Marcus, "in case you were wondering." Marcus fought the urge to jokingly say, `is that the same thing around here?' And instead, just nodded in acquiescence.

"Pleased to meet you," said Marcus to Pete.

"Pleased to meet you too", said Marcus.

"Well, what will you guys be having today," said Pete? "Do you want something Italian and fancy for Marcus here? I can do that too Aubrey, it's on the menu too," said Pete, pointing to a bleached wooden board behind him.

"No, we are both good," said Aubrey. "We are just going to have your normal iced coffee. Large cups please."

"Normal it is! Pete exclaimed.

There was no denying it, thought Marcus on the way back, the coffee was extremely good.

He wasn't sure what the taste was. Cinnamon? Vanilla? He had no idea.

"I have to hand it Pete," said Marcus, looking at the hut, "I didn't think the coffee would be anything special. There is no doubt though, that it is delicious. What does he put in it? Do you know?"

"It's a secret family recipe," said Aubrey. "He and Jenny have had that in their family for generations. I am glad you like it."

When they got back to the house, Aubrey went off to make the salad for the barbecue, while Marcus got some plates ready. Those sigils, or magic signs, or whatever they were, had made him curious. He resolved to ask Aubrey more about them. One thing in particular bothered him, especially given his years of experience in hiking and tracking. The grass around the fire pit had been trampled, and it looked like there had been lots of people there. Yet, Aubrey had specifically said that she had had no visitors, and that it had not rained for weeks. But, when Marcus checked last week's weather forecast on his phone, it showed heavy rain for two days last week. Why would she not tell him the truth about something like that? He shook his head. It probably was just her and the kids. The journey here with Ed had made him paranoid.

He decided to put it out of his mind and enjoy the barbecue. The food was laid out and ready to cook by the time the other guests arrived. The guests were Aubrey's uncle John and her eldest son, Landon, and his girlfriend Trina.

Marcus had stacked the wood ready for the fire to be lit, and then told Aubrey he was going for a shower. By the time he got out, he found the house empty. The guests, as well as Aubrey, Seth and Trina, were already standing out by the fire, which had been lit. Aubrey was busy cooking the meat over an open grill.

"We thought we would get started as the others arrived while you were in there," said Aubrey, rising to give him a kiss on the cheek, as Marcus approached.

"No problem," said Marcus, going straight to the fire. The night was not cold, but he felt a chill and he had always enjoyed the comfort of a fire.

"John," this is Marcus. "Marcus, this is John," said Aubrey.

"Hi," said Marcus, as he looked up at her uncle. Marcus was not small, standing around six feet, but John, at what Marcus guessed must be around six feet five, towered over him. He was broad too, with a ginger and grey peppered beard. He smiled at Marcus, and then proceeded to give him a hug. "Welcome to the family. That is the way we do things on my side of it anyway," said John.

"Thank you so much," said Marcus, "it is good to be here."

Landon, Aubrey's eldest, had obviously inherited his physique from his mother. He was average height, but muscular, Marcus could tell. He had the same dark auburn hair and dark skin as his mother. In contrast, Trina, his girlfriend, had almost white blond hair and very pale blue eyes. She was friendly enough when she was introduced to Marcus, but behind her eyes, he could sense something else. A type of nervousness? Was it as strong an emotion as fear? Why would she fear him? Maybe it was just teenage awkwardness, Marcus thought, and dismissed it.

As she prepared the food, Aubrey put some music on. Country folk singers yawled out a tune from the speakers. It was from a local band, Landon explained to him, not that he would have known who they were, even if they had been very famous. Marcus had hardly ever listened to country. Trina began serving the food. Nobody said thank you to Trina, except for Marcus, which struck him as odd. Being last in the queue for the food, Marcus said a loud and slightly exaggerated "thank you", as he took his plate from Trina. This caused her to widen her eyes in response, before she mumbled a "you are welcome."

"And now," it is time to sing the song to welcome Marcus," said Aubrey.

"Finally," said John to Marcus, "Aubrey said I couldn't have any of this, until we had done that, and who am I to argue with her."

John flashed a flask at Marcus. "The best moonshine in these parts", said John, then he added, "with a clear emphasis on the best."

The family then stood around the fire in a circle. They began singing and swaying as they did so. Only Trina remained outside it. She had retreated behind the serving table, and Marcus could barely make her out behind it.

From far away they always come,

They must be tested, and not undone,

They must be strong and bright and true,

For if they are not, they will end up in the ground, and be blue.

Oh, Mother make them promise!

Oh, mother make them promise!

Oh, mother make them promise!

Let him be the one.

Let it finally be done.

Yalwal nighrin partak!

Then they all turned to Marcus and clapped. John slapped him on the back, and handed him the bottle, encouraging him to swallow a big glug of moonshine, which he did.

Aubrey's eyes were glistening. As she came over to him and planted a firm, luscious kiss on the lips.

"That was great," said Marcus, but I have to ask, what were those words you spoke at the end? They sounded foreign. What language is that?

"That is Salbo, our local language. It's an ancient oral and magical language, which only a few families carry on around here. All the Salbo speakers know one another. There are only a few hundred of us at most. Few outsiders ever hear it. You are quite honored , in fact. If somebody outside the families asked after it, we would deny its existence."

"That is truly fascinating," said Marcus. "I would love to learn some of it."

"And you shall," replied Aubrey. "I hope."

Marcus wanted to ask more about the strange language, but was pulled away by John for another glug of moonshine.

"Hopefully we can go out fishing soon," said John, "I would love to take you."

"That would be great!" Said Marcus, "I have plenty of time right now given my teaching schedule, so whenever you can arrange it."

As he turned towards the fire, he saw that Aubrey was sprinkling paper squares on top of it.

As she was on the other side of the fire, he decided to ask John what she was up to.

"That's part of the ceremony," he explained in a casual tone. "We rid ourselves of past mistakes. It makes the passage of the new that much easier."

"Uh huh," said Marcus giving an understanding nod, when really, he didn't understand at all. The moonshine must be extremely strong, but he still had the presence of mind though, to stomp on one of the scraps of paper that had fluttered out of the fire. He waited until the others were distracted, and then picked it up, stuffing it in his pocket as he did so. Coming up from the ground, he caught Trina's eye. She looked at him almost pleadingly he thought, but said nothing to him at all.

He couldn't remember the party ending, but he was aware of a physical pressure on top of him. It must be Aubrey he thought, and then he felt something squeezing his neck.

...Just before he passed out.

Evil In Ollenberry

Marcus could remember virtually nothing of the night before, and he felt a little embarrassment as a consequence. They had had a barbecue sure, and some of Aubrey's family had come round, as well as Landon's girlfriend, he remembered that. He had forgotten everything else though. Everything. It must be that moonshine of her Uncle John's, he reasoned. He resolved not to drink that ever again.

He went outside to have a cigarette. He hated the fact that he still smoked, and every time he had one, he was furious with himself for still doing so, but on mornings like this he reasoned, he needed some clarity.

As he delved into his pocket, he pulled out a piece of paper. It was slightly charred around the edges, but there was a name on it, beautifully written, in bold dark letters: **Simon Cornish.**

Now, it came back to him. The business of the singing, that strange local language they spoke here that he had never heard of. All of it came back to him. He took a drag from the cigarette and considered his next move. How could he forget all the things that had happened last night? It didn't seem possible. Maybe it was that damn moonshine. He should discuss it with Aubrey, of course he should, he thought to himself. Not just yet, he thought. He would see what Ed thought of it all first. He would give him a call in the next few days.

Marcus pushed the piece of paper with the name back into his coat.

After breakfast, Aubrey suggested that they should get a coffee from Pete's, and then go into town. "You can grab some candy from that cute little shop, and there are other stores you can look at there too as you wander around. I want you to play a game with me if that's alright?"

"Sure," said Marcus. "What would you like me to do?"

"Well, she said I am going to choose seven stores in the town that you can visit. You have to choose three of them. I want you to get one thing from each store. I won't go into them myself. I don't want to influence you in any way. As I said, you have to pick one thing from each of them, barring the sweet shop, there you can get yourself a bag of whatever you like. Does that sound like fun?"

"In a way it does, I guess," said Marcus. "It also sounds a little weird too. Why would I do this? Does the game have any purpose to it?"

Aubrey laughed in response, and then she said. "Not at all my love. It's just a fun family tradition we sometimes play. After you have finished, you get to come back, and show me what you have got. Okay?"

"Okay," said Marcus. "I have to admit it sounds bizarre, but I am up for it."

"Great! Said Aubrey. "Now, there are just two more rules. Firstly, you must not bring me anything, and I really mean anything at all. I mean it it's part of the game."

"That's going to be very difficult to do Aubrey, I adore you. I just can't not get you anything."

"Babe, I want you to know that I am serious, very serious when I say this," said Aubrey sternly. "I will compromise a little. You can get me some liquorish from the sweet shop, but that is it. Are we clear?"

"We are clear," said Marcus, a little startled by her firmness. I will buy absolutely nothing at all but three items, which include something from the sweet shop."

"Good," said Aubrey, smiling again. The last thing is that you only have thirty minutes to choose your objects and get back to me with them. After that, you are done. If you don't return with three things, then you have to stick with what you have. Understood?"

"Yes, I understand." Said Marcus, who was clearly bemused at the strange game, but also, at the same time, looking forward to it for reasons he couldn't fathom.

Aubrey suggested that they have a coffee at Pete's to get him going, and Marcus readily agreed. He needed to get the fog out of his brain. Although Aubrey had presented this as some sort of game, he had a feeling that it had some sort of significance to it, that she wasn't telling him about. What could it be though? He wished he had Ed on the phone right now. He would call him after she had dropped him off, Marcus decided.

"What'll it be?" Said Pete. "A normal?"

"Just one normal, said Aubrey, "that's for me. Marcus is feeling a bit tired today though. He needs a special I think."

"Ohh a special," said Pete. "Coming right up."

"What's in a special?" Said Marcus to Aubrey.

"Nothing out of the ordinary," she replied. "Just a bit of extra boost. Just drink it quickly before you start your shopping, if you don't mind. Most of the places you might go into, won't let you bring drinks in. And you will need some clarity of mind to get your stuff, I think."

Marcus needed no encouragement to do that, and he readily gulped down the drink as fast as he could. Within a few minutes, he found himself to be hyper focused, indeed even the colors of the things around him as they travelled to the center of town seemed more vivid. Now, the greens of the trees and grass seemed to be almost glowing and shimmering, and even the birdsong seemed louder and more resonant. He could hear it even as they travelled down the road. He could never smell the tobacco on him, although Aubrey regularly complained that she could. Now though, it took on a pungent stale odor that repelled him.

Now, they got out of the car and walked towards the center of the crossroads that marked the center of town.

"Are you good?" said Aubrey.

"I am good," said Marcus. "I am ready."

"Well then, let me tell you which shops you can go to, she said. "The first one is obviously the sweet shop. I suggest you go there first. Don't eat any of the sweets you choose though. Please save them for later. After that, you can choose from the antiques shop, the auto mechanics, the butchers, the clothes shop, the mirror and paintings store, and the travel shop. Got it?"

"Yes," said Marcus, "I understand."

"You can only look from the outside though. Once you go inside, you are committed to getting something from that store."

"There are a lot of rules to this game, it seems," said Marcus.

Evil In Ollenberry

"There is just one more, said Aubrey, holding out her hand as she did so. "Gimme."

"Give you what?" said Marcus a little nervously. For some reason he went for the piece of paper with the name of Simon Cornish, that he had put in his pocket earlier.

"Your cellphone," said Aubrey. "I don't want you to google things to see what they are. No technological advantages. I want you to use your instinct to play the game. Use your emotions. Nothing else."

Marcus handed over his phone, without complaint.

"You still have your watch" Aubrey said, smiling and hugging him as she did so. "Imagine doing this without that and trying to guess the time."

"Yes, you are so generous, I am very grateful," said Marcus, with a touch of sarcasm in his voice.

"Ready?" Said Aubrey.

"Ready." Said Marcus.

"I will see you back at the car in thirty minutes then," said Aubrey.

The first place was the one he was looking forward to most, Marcus thought. He could happily spend the entire thirty minutes in the sweet shop. He opened the door. The place was exactly like the one from his increasingly distant childhood. The counter was a dark polished wood, and jars of delicious looking candies went from the floor to the ceiling of the little shop. So many, hundreds in fact, with names he had never heard of printed on the jars, like 'gooblestomp' and 'muck raker'. None of the names on the jars seemed to give him any clue as to the contents inside them. This was going to be harder than he imagined, he thought.

"How can I help you?" Said a very frail looking old lady, who suddenly appeared from behind the counter. She peered at him carefully from over half moon spectacles. She was wearing what looked like a pink overcoat, which almost drowned her, as Marcus estimated that she must be less than five feet tall.

"I am here to buy some sweets." Marcus mumbled.

"Of course you are, she chuckled. I am Marion, she said. Now, young man, please tell Marion what you would like." Marion! Marcus thought. Just like the old lady who he used to buy sweets off when he was a child. What a coincidence.

"I can't tell what the jars contain from the names, can you help me with that?"

"Well, that would take all day," Marion replied, "and I have a feeling that you don't have much time, eh?"

Marcus nodded in response. Could she know about the game, he considered. Then he dismissed the thought. That wasn't possible.

"What flavors do you like?" Said Marion.

"I probably like them all, except licorice. Said Marcus. "And I have to get some of that, anyway."

"Of course you do, dear," said Marion, smiling sweetly as she did so.

Here, let me help you, I will list some flavors, and you can tell me what you like best, okay?"

"Marshmallow, chocolate, spearmint, peppermint, ginger, molasses, cinnamon, vanilla, honey and coconut." Which of those are you attracted to most?"

"I have to pick three, said Marcus. "So, of those, I would probably choose Spearmint, honey and chocolate."

"Very good choices," said Marion. "I will get some down from the jars." With that, Marion grabbed a stool from behind the counter, and three paper bags.

"Can I help?" said Marcus.

"No, my dear," said Marion, "don't worry, I am way fitter than I look."

"Okay, I will just stand here and wait, if that's okay?" said Marcus.

"You do just exactly that," said Marion.

She turned and proceeded to pour the contents of three of the jars into their respective white paper bags. "There," she said, as she came down from the stool. "That should do it. That will be three dollars."

"Wow," said Marcus. "That's cheap. I don't know how you keep going with those prices."

"I don't do it for money, said Marion. "I could have retired a long time ago. I do it because I enjoy it. Even at my age, it's important to follow your passions. It's what keeps you alive, don't you think?"

"Yes, I can't argue with that," said Marcus. I wish everyday life didn't get in the way though. We all have bills to pay."

"It is so,so important, said Marion. "When you are my age, you won't remember the mundanities of life. They are like drinking water. Just plain and what you need to get through the day. You will remember though, how you felt, and what you saw."

Evil In Ollenberry

"That's very good advice said Marcus. "I have always tried my best to follow my passions, in fact,that is the main reason why I am here."

"I know dear, "said Marion. She seemed lost for a minute, as if she wanted to add something, but she just stared down at the counter. Marcus waited patiently until she spoke again, but there was nothing. With the silence becoming awkward, he eventually broke it by saying, "I am sorry, but I must be off now, I have some more shopping to do, and I don't have much time."

"I know, I know," said Marion," but before you go, let me at least tell you what my sweets are for? Okay?"

"I don't understand," said Marcus.

"I make these sweets myself, and they have meaning. You have chosen spearmint for speed, honey for healing and chocolate to make you feel good. Don't take too much, they are strong for sweets. And only use one bag per each full moon. Don't worry, they will keep. You will know when to eat them. And hopefully I will see you in three months' time."

"Will they really keep for three months?" said Marcus, and then he added, "my fiancé tells me that your sweets are exceptional. So, I am hoping I will see you well before three months ."

"They are exceptional. Very special indeed. So, keep them safe, and only eat them when you really need them. You will know when." said Marion.

"Okay, I shall," said Marcus, who by now was feeling a bit disturbed by his trip to the previously innocuous sweet shop.

"I am so glad," said Marion. "Good luck, and I hope I that I shall see you very soon indeed. You are kind, just what our little town needs."

"Thank you", said Marcus, "I will do my very best to meet people's approval."

Marcus wandered down the street, peering into the windows of the shops that he was allowed to go into as per the rules of the game. The butcher's looked unremarkable, with a couple of pigs hanging in the window, and some steaks and chickens on display in trays. That would be a nope then.

He only shot the briefest of glances at the auto repair shop. He had no interest in cars, and so he decided to dismiss it almost instantly.

There was a clothes shop, and with options narrowing, he decided that he could probably find something to wear from there, so he went inside.

The first thing he noticed was the smell. It smelled of musky animal, like a horse, maybe? Marcus thought. It also looked dirty. There was dust everywhere, like it had rarely been cleaned, or visited.

The whole place was brilliantly lit. There were lamps of all kinds everywhere, leading to every tawdry cranny being exposed. Within a few seconds, he considered turning around. Then he remembered what Aubrey had said. Once inside you are committed, so he really had no choice but to carry on and make the best of whatever he found. The place seemed deserted, which didn't surprise him, as he did wonder what type of customer might use this place. He wandered over to the racks.

Most of the clothing did not come as a single item, like a shirt or a pair of trousers, but rather as a complete outfit. One suit for example was from the 1930's, complete with a trilby. Another was an entire astronaut's costume complete with helmet. In the corner, there was even a suit of armor! Marcus was drawn to this and began examining it. Unlike the rest of the shop and clothing, it seemed highly polished.

"Hello", said a voice behind him. "Hello".

Marcus swung around to see a small rotund man standing behind him. He was immaculately dressed, sporting pinstripe pants, a red waistcoat, and a white shirt, and spotted bow tie. Most oddly, he also was wearing what looked like a red fez, on the top of his head.

"Allow me to introduce myself, sir." said the man, speaking with a British accent. "My name is Giles. I am the shopkeeper. How can I help you?"

Marcus had a myriad of questions from just looking at the man, but he decided to focus on the task.

"Hello Giles, I am Marcus. "I have to get an outfit, and I am in a hurry."

"Of course, you are sir, but do not worry. I can help. Is there any particular one you are drawn to? The suit of armor perhaps? Nothing can get through it, and it is surprisingly lightweight, as you will see if you purchase it."

"I can't afford a suit of armor," said Marcus, "as amazing as it looks."

"It is three dollars, sir", said Giles.

"Three dollars? That's amazing! Really?" said Marcus, astounded. I paid a dollar each for three bags of sweets, in the shop just down the road, and I thought that was a great deal. But, three dollars for a suit of armor! That's insane! How do you make a profit?"

"It's not about the profit, sir, it's about the passion." Replied Giles.

I can understand that, but why isn't the place overrun? I mean, it should be. All of these outfits should have been bought out by now."

"I am selective as to my customers, sir". said Giles.

Marcus wanted to debate that point further with the shopkeeper, not least as he had been able to walk straight in, but he needed to focus on the task. The suit of armor was amazing. Much as he liked it, what would he do with it though? Where would he put it? Aubrey's house was pretty cramped already.

He glanced around, trying to pick something. Then he saw it. A Cowboy costume. What a costume it was though. A black suit, with silver stirrups on the boots, with a gun holster containing two pistols. There was a crisp white shirt, underneath a beautifully embroidered silver waistcoat.

Marcus turned to the shopkeeper and said, "I will have that, even though I won't have time to try it on."

"It will fit sir, don't worry." Said Giles.

Marcus looked at the shopkeeper quizzically, before saying slowly "and this entire outfit, including the hat, is three dollars?"

"Yes, it is." said Giles, passively.

Evil In Ollenberry

"Is everyone in on this game I am playing with Aubrey?" said Marcus.

"I mean, I know you guys are in a small town and all, but this seems like you all went to a lot of trouble for, for what exactly?"

"I don't know what you mean?", said Giles quietly.

"Of course you don't," said Marcus, his tone clearly indicating that he meant the exact opposite. "I will take it."

"Very good sir," said Giles. "That will be three dollars."

Marcus handed the money to Giles and began striding out of the door.

"Just one last thing sir, said Giles.

"Yes," said Marcus.

"Don't let her wash it before you wear it. You must wear it as it is now."

"Forgive me, but I would like to wash it. You must know, that's what I am going to do before I wear it."

"Please don't sir," said Giles. " It will dilute the power. Wear it as it is. That's all I can say."

"Okay," said Marcus, He nodded in agreement, but did not understanding anything at all about what Giles had just said.

Evil In Ollenberry

There was one more shop to visit, before he had to get back to Aubrey. He had just less than ten minutes left, so he decided to be purposeful. He headed straight for the antiques shop. He must, he reasoned, be able to pick up something quickly from there, whatever it was. He ran to the opposite side of the street and pushed open the door to the shop.

The antiques store was immaculate. In complete contrast to the clothing shop. The lighting inside the shop was extremely bright, with shiny silver and brass objects that gleamed so much, that they actually hurt his eyes. Marcus squinted as he looked at them. The shop also had a very strong smell. What was it? Marcus thought to himself. Vanilla? Undoubtedly. It seemed to cling to him already, like it was burying itself into his pores. He was glad he didn't hate the smell.

Now, a woman in a skintight red dress strode towards him. To say she was voluptuous, was an understatement. She had huge, almost cartoon like, breasts which contrasted with her tiny waist. She wore no jewelry that Marcus could see. She had on black stiletto shoes, the heels of which must have been around six inches tall. Even with those on, she strode towards Marcus purposefully. Her long brown hair was combed to one side, and she wore bright red lipstick, in contrast to her pale white skin. She was certainly attractive, but in a sleazy kind of way, Marcus considered.

"Hello, the woman purred, "my name is Emily. How can I help you today?"

"I am looking for something, something that I apparently might need, but I have no idea what it is." said Marcus. "I know that sounds vague, but I haven't much time."

Emily smiled at him, and then came closer. Very close indeed, so that her lips almost touched his ear. Marcus froze, unsure of what to do. Then, she purred "if you haven't much time, why don't you just choose from the table over there? Smaller objects are on there. You can carry whatever you pick easily. You could choose from that table, and be out before you know it."

"Great idea," said Marcus. Easing away from the woman as he spoke. "I will do just that."

He walked towards the center of the room. In the middle of it, there were a variety of objects arranged on a beautiful carved wooden black table, which Marcus guessed must be around twelve feet across.

He picked up a silver snuff box from it and twisted it in his hand. It was ornately carved, with long silver spirals, which twisted into such small patterns that the detail became beyond his eye.

Evil In Ollenberry

"That one is so useful to heighten the senses," said Emily. "It shows things that can't be seen by the human eye".

Marcus didn't have time to ask her how a snuff box could do that, but he wished he could. The surreal shopping trip would no doubt stay with him for years, but right now he needed to worry about picking up what he needed. "What are you drawn to?" said Emily. "You can close your eyes if you like?" Now she was behind him, and so close that he felt her breasts brush against his back.

He picked up a carved horn. It was varnished and brilliantly white, with a little golden chain and clip attached to it.

"That's for warning you of danger," said Emily. You never know, it could come in handy."

"I hope not, but it certainly is a lovely piece." said Marcus.

He was about to take it, when he saw the watch. It was unremarkable at first, with a rough looking brown leather strap. As Marcus scanned it though, he could see that it was in fact, beautifully made. It was studded with tiny rubies and sapphires, with golden hands which pointed to the numbers.

What really drew him though, was the tiny picture in the middle of it. There was a skeleton on one side holding a scythe, and what looked like a warrior of some kind directly opposite him holding a sword. In between the two of them was a little clock face, with the hands it seemed, stuck on midnight.

"I will take it!" said Marcus.

"That's a great choice, said Emily. "I am very impressed. It is a beautiful piece. And after all, time is fluid. Our choices and perceptions make it what it is."

"To a degree, I guess", said Marcus. "I don't think I can change my past, but I can change the way I feel about it. The future, however, is exciting. I can't wait for that."

"I have no doubt that your future will be interesting," said Emily. "No doubt at all." Then she added. "Let the watch bond with you. I suggest you put it on now. Don't let anyone else handle it before you do so."

"Okay," said Marcus. He slid his G shock watch off, and placed the antique watch on his wrist. It felt cool, but not uncomfortable.

"Excellent," said Emily, that will be just three dollars."

"Of course, it will." Marcus replied. "Aubrey certainly has gone to a lot of trouble for this game."

Marcus, saw Emily's eyes narrow just for a second, before they returned to their normal shape.

"Believe me when I tell you I am only here to help you, Marcus." said Emily.

"I didn't give you my name," said Marcus. There was no intensity to his statement, just curiosity in his tone.

"I hope I see you soon", said Emily. I am sure you must run now though. I would guess you only have a few minutes to get back to that Aubrey before your time runs out, and you don't want to lose your objects, I have no doubt that you will need them."

Marcus knew he didn't have time to ask her what she meant, so, he merely replied, "thank you Emily", and hurried out of the door.

"My pleasure," said Emily, blowing him a kiss as she did so.

Marcus hurried towards Aubrey's car. He could see it parked at the end of the street. He couldn't run, the cowboy boots and outfit would have made that awkward, and he had enough time. He was so focused on Aubrey's car, that he didn't see the old woman cutting across his path, until she was almost right on top of him. He had to work hard to avoid crashing right into her.

She was stooped over and seemed to be resting on a long black wooden cane. Yet she had come out of nowhere and crashed right into him.

"I can help," said the old lady.

"I can help," she repeated, "but there isn't much time. She can't see me, but you absolutely MUST not tell her I have spoken to you. The family members are all ancient."

"Uh huh", said Marcus, looking at his brand-new watch. Twenty seconds left.

"I am sorry, but if you are part of the game, a distraction or something, then it isn't going to work."

Marcus moved to go past the old woman, but as he did so, she grabbed his shoulder. Her grip was surprisingly hard considering how frail she looked, and it startled him.

"When you need me", said the old woman, "call out `Katy come get me`, three times, and I will be there. Do it outside, and it must be three times. You will know when. And don't tell Aubrey! She isn't what she seems!"

"Sure", said Marcus as he ran towards the car. He was on it now, and barely heard the last few words the old woman shouted as he past her, so determined was he to get in the car.

Aubrey was beaming at him when he slid in. "Phew, just in time. Well done babe. It seemed like you got pulled up just before you got to the car. What was that about?"

So, Marcus reasoned, Aubrey really hadn't seen the old lady. Or maybe it was part of this bizarre game? He had no idea. He decided he would play along though.

"I thought I had forgotten one of the packets of sweets", said Marcus." I was just checking to see if I had them all."

"You wouldn't have had time to go back and get it, even if you had", said Aubrey, " but I understand. Did you like the sweetshop?"

"Yes, I loved it." said Marcus. "It was almost exactly like the one I remembered from my childhood, and Marion was very sweet indeed. I got three packets."

"Well, don't tell me what they are," said Aubrey," but you can tell me what shops you went to."

"First, I went into the sweet shop. What a great place that is. It was almost exactly like the one from my childhood."

"Wonderful," said Aubrey. "Don't tell me what packets you got, that is part of the game."

Evil In Ollenberry

"Okay", said Marcus. He was confused. He thought the game was over, and was about to press her on the subject. Aubrey however, seemed excited and her voice was raised. She shouted the next question "What other shops did you go to?"

"First the clothes shop, and then the antique shop." Marcus replied.

Aubrey frowned. " Mmm. You saw Emily. Attractive, isn't she?"

Marcus perceived that this was a loaded question, and he had to answer carefully. "Umm yes, she is. Not the sort of woman I would be interested in, and I did my best to get out of there as quickly as possible."

"I am sure you did." said Aubrey. "I can smell the vanilla , that she drowns herself and that shop of hers in. I can't stand that smell. I hope you don't mind if we go back home now, and you take a shower when we get back? I think I am allergic to vanilla. It actually makes me physically sick."

"Of course," Marcus replied. "I am sorry the smell is so bad. If I had known, I wouldn't have gone in the antique shop."

"I could never restrict your choices," said Aubrey." That would be cheating. Anyway, I can see where you went to next, the clothes shop! That's a very cool cowboy outfit."

"Yes, I am really happy with it." said Marcus.

"What did you get from the ever-fragrant Emily's shop then?" Aubrey asked.

"This watch, isn't it beautiful? Marcus replied.

"It really is," said Aubrey slowly, twisting his wrist to examine it." I don't remember seeing anything like it, when I was in her shop. Mind you, it's been a long time since I was there."

Once they got back, Marcus headed for the shower. " I can wash your clothes now if you like?" said Aubry.

"Yes please,"said Marcus, "that's very kind of you, but you don't have to do that. I can do it myself."

"Not at all, I need to rid both you and my house of that vanilla smell," she replied. "Here, hand me that cowboy outfit, I will get it out of that too."

"There is no need," said Marcus. "I promise it doesn't smell at all."

"It can't hurt to wash it though," said Aubrey pressing the subject.

"The shopkeeper, a man called Giles, told me not to. I am going to respect his wishes," Marcus replied.

Evil In Ollenberry

Marcus saw just a flicker of irritation pass across Aubrey's face, before she covered it up. "He should not have told you that", she said flatly." No matter though. You are right, it doesn't smell. Let's leave it be. I will let you grab you shower now," Aubrey said, "playfully slapping Marcus on the ass as he headed towards the shower."

"Aubrey, I have a million questions about this game that we are playing. The whole town seemed in on it, the shops were creepy as hell there were no other customers, and everything was three damned dollars!"

Marcus realized that he was sounding loud and exasperated now, so he stopped himself. "I am sorry my love, I am just a bit confused. I guess with the move and all."

"Don't worry", Aubrey said soothingly. "I will answer what I can after dinner, when the kids have gone to bed. Is that okay?"

"Sure," said Marcus. Her comments though, only made him speculate even more intensely. What was it that she had to say. He thought was little more than an amusing game, that she had to give him such a lengthy explanation for? What the hell was going on here?

Dinner was good. Aubrey made some chicken breast, which she had sauteed in a thick barbecue sauce. The recipe, it turned out, was another `family secret`. How many of these family secrets were there, Marcus pondered to himself.

He started to feel sleepy almost immediately afterwards. He fought sleep however, for he was determined to ask Aubrey about the game, and its implications. By the time the kids had gone to bed though, his eyelids were so heavy that he was looking at Aubrey thorough slits.

"Hey Babe, I know you are getting tired. I can see it. Is there anything you would like to ask me before you do fall asleep?"

"Yes," said Marcus. "Please tell me about the game. At first, I thought it was just a bit of fun between the two of us, but now I realize that the whole town is involved, and frankly it became a bit creepy and strange. There were no other customers in the shops. Everything, and I do mean everything, including antiques and even an immaculate suit of armor, was three dollars. All of the shopkeepers were in on our game, it seems. What is going on?"

Aubrey laughed loudly at this, and then she said. "I am sorry it was so elaborate. And yes, they were all in on it. I know, to you, it seemed rather strange. You are new in town and special to me, that's all. I asked them to role play it for us, to make it more intense and fun. It all worked out really well. I thought, I am sorry though, if it creeped you out a bit. That wasn't my intention."

"What was your intention though Aubrey. I am still not really understanding it. And do I have to return the watch I got from the antiques store, and the cowboy outfit? They can't be worth three dollars." Said Marcus.

"Not at all", said Aubrey, "They are gifts from Emily and Giles. I am from a very old family, and family names count around here. They know how important you are to me, and they are happy for me. Everyone has been welcoming to you, haven't they? They just want to see me happy. All people want is to wish us well."

"That is very kind of them." said Marcus.

"There really are sweet people around here," said Aubrey. "You will grow to love them. Now, you have been ready for bed for a long time. Do you have any more questions before we go?"

"No, I am good." said Marcus.

Aubrey took his hand and they walked into the bedroom. He didn't remember taking off his clothes, but when he woke up, he was naked.

CHAPTER THREE

-Shall We Dance-

"You are going to be sacrificed," said Ed. "It is difficult to find middle aged virgins. Aubrey knew when she met you that you were a virgin. That whole creepy town is going to gather around and sing a song in that strange fucking language of theirs, and that will be it."

Marcus had awoken early and crept out of the house while Aubrey was sleeping, phoned Ed, and told him in detail what had happened since he had been dropped off.

"Is that your best answer?" said Marcus in response, his voice thick with humor. " Do you want to come and see the bonfire? I think I might suggest to them that they need two virgins, to make those flames burn really high, and that I know the perfect person for that."

Ed laughed at this, and then said, "You know, I am just joking, but in all seriousness, that does sound as creepy as hell. I would watch your back. That whole shopping business game is weird, and that singing around the fire, and burning names. I have no idea what that means, but it seems to be that it would go way beyond some sort of local custom. It sounds like some sort of modern-day witchcraft or something, that they are all in on."

"What would you do if you were me?" said Marcus.

Ed sighed before responding. "I would leave. Pack my bags and not look back. I know you love her, but to me, it's a place I would not want to be around."

"I get it Ed, I really do", said Marcus in response, "but on the other hand I feel like I just got here, and now because of what is at the moment harmless eccentric behavior, I am thinking of leaving. Nobody has harmed me. Everyone has been kind to me."

"I knew you would say that", said Ed, "and I get it. I want you to be happy, you deserve it. Look, let's strike a compromise, shall we? What was the name of that guy on the piece of paper? Simon Cornish, was it?"

"Yes, that's right," said Marcus.

"I have a good buddy who is a private detective, a guy called Dan. We met when I was studying for my criminology degree. Let me see if he can find out anything about this guy. He owes me a favor. Just a name isn't much to go on, but he might come up with something", said Ed.

"That sounds like a really good idea," said Marcus.

Evil In Ollenberry

"Good," said Ed. "Watch your back, and if you need me, at any time of the day or night, don't hesitate to give me a call."

"I promise I will," said Marcus. "Be safe on the road."

"You be safe too,"said Ed, before adding, "and keep that virginity of yours, intact. It's a precious thing."

"I will, "replied Marcus laughing, "it's good that us virgins stick together."

The conversation with Ed, had given him a bit of focus, Marcus considered. The game had been bizarre but harmless. And Ed would have his friend check up on that Simon Cornish guy.

The only thing that troubled him was the old woman who said she could help him, that Katy. How did she fit into this. He had not told Aubrey about her. He wasn't proud of keeping secrets from Aubrey. She had been nothing but kind to him, but it was just too weird not to be a little suspicious. So, he would keep Katy to himself...at least for now.

"Morning Babe," said Aubrey. She was up and dressed by the time he came back in the house after he spoke to Ed, and she handed him a cup of coffee, as she spoke. "What have you been up to?" She said nonchalantly.

"I have been speaking to Ed," Marcus replied. "I thought I would call him outside, as I didn't want to wake you up."

"That's thoughtful of you," said Aubrey. "What did he have to say? Did you tell him about the game we played yesterday?"

"Yes, I did," said Marcus. "And he thinks that you want to sacrifice me, as I am a virgin."

Aubrey laughed deeply. She had a very deep laugh, so loud at times, that it almost seemed like it was shaking the walls.

"Now we both know that's not true", she said, arching her eyebrows as she spoke. Then she added, "I have always liked Ed. He always comes across as a fun guy."

"Indeed he is," Marcus replied. "He said to tell you hi."

"I hope he comes to see us soon," said Aubrey.

"I hope so too," Marcus replied. "I forgot to ask him when he will next be in the area, but I will when we next speak."

"Good," said Aubrey. "Hey, I had a couple of ideas. There is a full moon coming up tomorrow. A restaurant in town is having a party to celebrate it. They do it once a month and have special offers. Would you like to go?"

"Sure," said Marcus," that sounds like it would be fun."

"Great!" she replied. "And today, I have a little treat in store for you, just a little one. There is an old cornfield a few miles from here, it backs onto some woods where I used to play when I was a kid. What do you think about going up there and going into the corn field like you wanted to? "

"I know that a lot of farmers might get pretty nasty if they catch you in their fields. These days as well, a lot of them have cameras. That one however is owned by old Jessop. The corn isn't ready to ripen yet, and the field is way away from his farmhouse, so we shouldn't have any problems at all with him," said Aubrey

"Yeah, that sounds ideal," said Marcus. "Let's do it."

"I am so glad!" Aubrey responded, "just give me twenty minutes to feed and water the chickens, and we can be gone."

Aubrey wasn't a morning person, Marcus had known this for quite some time, and as such he tended to dance around her a bit to avoid her grumpy moods in the morning. Today however, she seemed very upbeat, and he was happy and glad.

Evil In Ollenberry

"What are we going to do when we get there?" said Marcus as they drove towards the field. "I want to take a few photos of me at the edge of it, and maybe inside it for a laugh. I know my friends will make a few `Children of the corn` comments when they see them, but otherwise I don't really need anything else."

"I thought you would say that, but we are going to have much more fun than that," Aubrey replied. "We are going to play a game."

"Oh no, not another game! said Marcus, throwing his hands up in mock drama as he did so. "Is the whole town in on this one too?"

"Haha!" Replied Aubrey, "no, just you and me, this time. And it will be fun, I promise. No stress. You know how I like games."

"Okay," I will indulge you said Marcus. "What are the rules of this one then?"

"It isn't complicated at all really, said Aubrey. " I am going to stand in the field, and you have to find me. It's as simple as that."

"That simple," said Marcus, before adding, "and is there anything else I should know?"

"No," said Aubrey, "that's it."

"I can't see what's in it for me," he said humorously, "so how about this. I have thirty minutes to find you. If I can't in that time, then I have to clean the chickens out for a week."

"Okay," said Aubrey.

"Wait, I haven't finished yet, "said Marcus, "but if I find you then I get to make mad passionate love to you tonight. Do we have a deal?"

"Absolutely!" said Aubrey laughing, "let the games begin!"

"Okay," said Aubrey. "It's 11.30, when it reaches noon, we are done. If you find me before then, then you get yours, agreed?"

"Agreed," said Marcus.

"I will win this game, I am sure of it," said Aubrey.

"You certainly have home advantage, I will admit that," said Marcus. "I am going to try my best though. Just remember though Aubrey, you can't move. You have to stay where you are, once you are in position, otherwise I don't stand a chance of finding you."

"Okay," said Aubrey, in mock reluctance.

Marcus had agreed on giving Aubrey a couple of minutes to get in position. He looked at the hands on his antique watch intently. He was going to give her that exact one hundred and twenty seconds, that's all.

Evil In Ollenberry

As he did so, though, the face of the watch startled him though. The hands on the circle which had previously remained stuck, now pointed to the skeleton. He was not overly superstitious, but he did pay some attention to omens, and he didn't like that.

There were two little winding mechanisms on the side of the watch, and now Marcus turned the smaller one which he guessed corresponded to the circle containing the skeleton and the warrior. He was right, and the moment he did so, the arms moved directly towards the warrior.

Two minutes was up. Time to look for Aubrey.

Marcus stepped into the corn field, and as he did so, his first instinct was to crouch low. He quickly stood up though, as he realized that this was the wrong approach. The corn was not fully ripened yet, and in most places, he could see right over the top of it. It was Aubrey who must be crouching, and given the fact that she could stay comfortable squatting, even while they were just casually chatting, she would probably be able to maintain this position for the entire thirty minutes.

So, he just stood up, and began moving through it. Slowly at first. Then he sped up pace, until he realized that moving too quickly, or running was almost impossible given the thickness of the stalks. He would have to wade and look, wade and look, until he found her, if he found her. The field was massive though, and he began to think that this might be a hopeless task. The cleaning out of the chickens would not be so bad, he thought. He could manage that if need be. Twenty minutes left. He decided to head for the middle of the field, stopping occasionally to listen for any sounds, any clue as to where she might be. If he had been Aubrey, and it really was a game, then he would have given her a little clue. Aubrey was highly competitive, and so far, there was nothing.

Then, he heard it. Just briefly. A little whistle. Unmistakably human, in the far-left corner of the field. He headed towards it now as quick as he could. When he first heard the rushing sound behind him, he thought it might just be the wind, and so he ignored it. He kept pushing on towards the whistling sound. Then he heard a crashing sound.

He swung around instinctively, and saw to his horror, some sort of giant creature heading directly towards him. He couldn't see it properly, as the corn buried most of the features of its body, but he could see that it was heading directly at him. Black-brown hair, he thought to himself. And then it roared, a guttural angry sound, straight from its belly. It was bear!

"Aubrey, a bear, a bear is coming. Get back to the car! Get out of here!" He shouted, but there was no response.

He ducked down into the corn, and turned at the sharpest angle he could. Crouched down, he ran towards the opposite direction from where he had last seen the bear. Then he went still. The bear rushed past him. It was so big, it felt like the ground shook as it did so. Almost breathless, he gave it a couple of seconds until he stood up again.

First, he looked in the direction it had gone. Then he scanned around, trying to see if it had turned. There was nothing. The car was about 200 yards away he reckoned, it was difficult to be sure. But he didn't see Aubrey in or around the car.

Hopefully, the bear had run off. Bears were very unlikely to attack people, he thought. Maybe something had just startled it, and he just happened to be unlucky enough to be caught in its path.

"Aubrey!" He shouted, "Aubrey! Are you okay?"

He heard a roar, which seemed to be coming from the direction the car was in, and then he saw the black and brown monster hurtling towards him.

This time, he decided to veer in the opposite direction, and it worked. The bear passed him.

He waited again before standing up. And looked around. Was it hunting him, he reasoned? If so, why? Then he remembered the sweets. Of course, that must be it. It must be attracted to the sweets. They were only in paper bags, the bear would easily be able to smell them. He would leave them here. And this time, creep out towards the car slowly. The bear had only swung around last time, when he had called out, he reasoned.

He moved forward excruciatingly slowly. He heard nothing but silence. He was sure the bear might hear his panting, but there was nothing. Just make progress, he said to himself. Just make progress. Aubrey never locked her car doors. Once he got there, he would be fine. He just hoped she had escaped. From her lack of response though, it seemed that she had. Hopefully, she was running for the authorities right now.

"Marcus! Marcus!" It was Aubrey. Keeping low, he moved to a place where she could see him. Aubrey was standing with her uncle, by the car. He was holding a shotgun. Both of them were peering into the field, searching for him.

"Run towards us babe," shouted Aubrey. "We have you covered."

"Take the damn sweet," said a voice suddenly.

"What," said Marcus?

"Take the damn sweet", repeated the voice. "The spearmint sweet, that gives you speed. You heard what Marion said."

Was that the voice of the old woman, that Katy? Marcus thought. It certainly sounded like her.

"Do what I say," said the voice with increasing urgency. "You don't want to be eaten alive, do you? And you know that this situation is unnatural, so what have you to lose? Do it! Do it now!"

Marcus could agree with the voice on that. There were very few bears in Ohio generally, and certainly not grizzlies. Yet here one was, charging at him the moment he stepped into the cornfield. He grabbed a spearmint sweet from the bag and crunched into it.

"Good," said the voice. "Now, when I tell you, run! Not when she does, you understand. When I do! You got that?"

"Yes, I have got it," said Marcus.

"Marcus! Marcus!" Shouted Aubrey. Marcus stood up now, and as he did so, the bear did too. It was directly behind him, less than ten feet away. The car he reckoned, was one hundred and twenty feet away. Bears run much faster than humans. He would have to be an Olympic sprinter to make it. And he wasn't that.

"Run! Run right towards us!" Shouted Aubrey. "We have you covered!"

"Run to the left!" Shouted the voice. "Do it now!"

Marcus ran towards the left of the field, pounding through the corn. The bear swung around behind him, giving him a precious half second of time, before it charged again.

He ran now, bursting through the corn. He felt his lungs sear with pain, as he wrenched himself forward, he could hear shouting, but it was making no sense to him. He could only hear was the roar of the bear as it came closer.

Then, his breathing suddenly became effortless, and he became lighter, much lighter. He seemed to be gliding through the corn, indeed it barely seemed to be moving as he rushed past it. Despite the peril he was in, he was enjoying himself, which was bizarre.

He rushed towards Aubrey and her Uncle John, who were stood on the very edge of the field. John had his shotgun raised, he could see that, and it was pointed in the direction of the bear. Amazingly, he was making ground on the bear. It seemed to be farther behind him.

"Shoot it! Shoot the fucking bear!" he shouted at John.

A shot rang out, and as it did so, he brushed past Aubrey and John. He was unable to stop running. He tried. But, as he looked down at his legs, they just kept on steamrolling along. It seemed like they were separate entities, not part of his own body. He had already crossed two fields and was still going.

"Focus," said Katy. "Imagine your legs to be stuck in mud. Really thick mud. You can't move, no matter how hard you try."

Marcus imagined wading through a swamp. Now the mud was getting thicker. Now his legs couldn't move. He felt himself slowing down, until finally he stopped, and instantly wretched.

He looked around. Aubrey and her uncle were mere dots in the distance. From what he could make out, they were waving to him, so they must have seen him. He slumped to the ground. He was exhausted. He would wait here for a while. Just rest. That's what he needed to do, until they got here.

He heard the car revving up and heading towards him. They would be here soon, and the bear must be gone. There was certainly no sign of it in the open fields.

"You did really well," said the voice," except for not calling me!"

"Not calling you?" Marcus said. "I am confused?"

"You did not say, 'Katy come get me,' three times in a row. Like I told you to," said the voice.

"I am sorry, but this is too bizarre," said Marcus. "I am talking to a disembodied voice in a field, after making an Olympic sprint to avoid a giant grizzly bear that shouldn't even exist here."

"Yet you know what happened," said Katy. "As weird as it is, this is all real. And, now you know, that you can trust me. I will help you. You can win."

"Just what exactly am I supposed to win here?" said Marcus. "...and what if I want to get the hell out of here? I think I should just fucking leave this town, and get away from all this crazy shit."

"They won't let you. After winning this, you might be valuable to them. You might very well be the one that they need." Said Katy.

"I don't give a shit what anyone in this crazy town needs, I am getting the fuck out of here," said Marcus. "They are trying to kill me!"

"Don't let them know your feelings. Act normal with Aubrey, or they will kill you. Contact me when you are sure that you are alone. And, whatever you do," said Katy, "do not say that I helped you. It is your only chance."

"Oh babe!" Shouted Aubrey. "Are you okay?" She and John were helping him to his feet now. Marcus staggered at first, before he stood up, and hugged her.

"I can't believe what just happened!" said Aubrey.

"And that run," added John "that was quite something. You were like a damn athlete."

"I think it must have been all the adrenaline," Marcus replied. "I have heard it can make people do amazing things when they are in mortal danger, like I was." Then he added, "where is the bear?"

"Darndest thing," said John. "I fired a shot straight at it, and it just disappeared! Or at least seemed to. Then we jumped in the car to get you. I have no idea where it went."

"It's a real menace! And a creature like that shouldn't even be in Ohio. We need to tell the authorities and get them to put out a press release. Anyone could be killed by that thing, and we must make sure people are safe!" Marcus explained, before collapsing into a coughing fit.

"Don't worry, my love," said Aubrey. "We will take care of it, won't we Uncle John?"

"Yes," said John. "I will get straight on it. You get him back home Aubrey. He needs to rest."

"Yes of course I will," said Aubrey. "Come on Marcus, let's get you home."

In the car on the way back, Aubrey was talking, but Marcus wasn't listening. The horror of what just happened had left him feeling crushed. He had to get out of here. How though? He must keep up the pretense to Aubrey, that he wanted a future here. He had to make her believe, that he felt it wasn't her fault.

How would he escape though? He didn't have a car. He had brought all of his belongings with him. He didn't want to part with all of his stuff. He felt desperate and alone.

"We are back now," said Aubrey soothingly."Why don't you just rest. I will make you some of my family's special herbal tea. That will calm you down."

Marcus didn't want to sound suspicious, so he gave the blandest response he could. "That sounds good," he said. He didn't want the tea, but he felt he had no choice but to drink some.

The tea, or whatever was in it, knocked him straight out. Again, in what he guessed was the middle of the night, he felt a writhing on top of him. He didn't know what it was, but it felt good, so he didn't resist it. He felt himself come, and heard a sigh in response to his soft moan.

When he woke up, it was morning, and Aubrey was there lying next to him, snoring loudly.

He slipped out of bed, and out of the front door.

"Get the fuck out of there, now!" said Rebecca.

Marcus's sister was always direct. "I have no idea what is going on there, but whatever it is, is insane! You are in danger. You must protect yourself!"

"I can't just leave without my stuff though. I have no transport, I am two hours drive from the nearest airport, and there aren't even any taxis here. I am screwed. I will have to walk out of here with just a backpack on if I do that." Said Marcus.

"Better that than be carried out of there in a coffin," said Rebecca. "I have never liked that damn Aubrey. I always thought that there was something `off` about her. Now I know it for sure. Why don't you contact your friend Ed, and arrange for him to come and pick you up? In the meantime, try and get out of the town. Do anything that takes you away from her and her family."

"I told Ed, that I would call him tomorrow, and I will. I will see what he can arrange. There is a guy here called Rusty, who has a lot of information on Bigfoot. He is really into Bigfoot research, which you know fascinates me too. I am hoping that he could give me some ideas for locations. It would keep both me and Aubrey busy. She is far more into the paranormal, as you know, but I reckon she would go for it."

"Okay, that's a good plan," said Rebecca. "Message me every day though. If I don't hear from you every single day, I am calling in the cavalry. I mean it."

"How are you feeling?" said Aubrey sweetly, handing him some tea as she did so. "Yesterday was quite a day. I am sure you are still feeling a little bruised by it all."

"Yes, I am, both mentally and physically," said Marcus. "I can't quite believe what happened."

"Neither can I," said Aubrey. "A bear! Of all things a bear! A grizzly bear! Isn't that amazing!" There was clear excitement in her voice as she said it.

"I think the word I would use would be horrifying, but I take your point," said Marcus.

"I am so sorry that happened to you, babe," said Aubrey, "but if there is an upside to it, you are now quite the local hero."

"What do you mean?" said Marcus.

"The whole town is talking about it now. They are having a fancy party soon, and you are going to be the guest of honor!"

"Really?" said Marcus, "all because I ran away from the bear?"

"You didn't just run away, you fooled it, and survived an attack. That's very rare. Very few people get to do that! You are a hero!" As she said this, she flung her arms around him, and kissed him passionately as she did so.

He responded, and kissed her in turn, with equal passion. Despite the situation he found himself in, he was very drawn to her physically. He had been from the moment he set eyes on her.

She smiled and then pulled away just enough so that she could see his face. "I thought you could have a bit of an easy morning and just rest today, if that's okay?"

"That sounds great," Marcus replied.

"After that though, I have some good news for you! You remember me telling you about Tate's, the big hardware store in town? Well, old man Tate heard about what happened with the bear. He called me while you were out talking to your sister. He would like to see you this afternoon at three, for an interview! As luck would have it, they have a sales position open. What do you think about that?"

"I still have my online teaching," said Marcus." but I know that's only part time. I don't know anything about hardware, but I am willing to give it a go."

"Wonderful!" said Aubrey. "I thought after lunch we could head out to the library and print off some copies of your resume to hand in at your interview, is that okay?"

"Yes, that works well for me," replied Marcus. I have always liked wandering around libraries as well."

"Good!" said Aubrey. "Well, our library is old. Nineteenth century, I think. It's in great condition. I am sure you will enjoy it."

The library was unusually ornate for a small town, thought Marcus as they pulled up to it.

The roof was painted white, and very angular. The two sides of it met in a sharp curve, which was decorated with a huge golden ball. The stairs leading up to the entrance were polished white marble.

Particularly striking though, were the gargoyles, one black and one white. They stood on either side of the stairs, guarding the entrance to it. Their faces were impassive and neutral.

As Marcus stood back to take a photo of the library's outside, Aubrey said "So, you are impressed by our little old library then?"

"I have never seen anything like it," Marcus replied. "It's so ornate, and these carvings must have cost a fortune."

"We value learning and family, "said Aubrey. "I was always taught that at school. These days, you can get almost everything on the Internet I know. Not quite everything though."

"I would agree," said Marcus. "There is something about the feel and smell of a book. I love plunging into them and getting lost in the words."

"Since you live here now, we will be able to get you a library card soon," said Aubrey. "For now though, you can have a quick look around while a get a couple of copies of your resume printed off, is that okay?"

"Sure," Marcus replied, "I am happy to wander around and check out the place."

"Okay," said Aubrey, "You go and do that, and I will come and find you in a few minutes."

Evil In Ollenberry

Marcus held the door open for Aubrey, who slipped past him, before heading for the front desk.

The library was just as ornate inside as outside, Marcus thought. A plush thick blue carpet weaved around the polished wooden bookcases. Green studded leather chairs and couches peppered the two large rooms, that were visible from the entrance. The ceiling was very high and painted a brilliant reflective white.

He walked to the carousel in front of him and picked up the first book that he came across. The title read: ` A Sheep Buyers guide`. The two other books next to it, were about tractor maintenance and how to breed ducks. None of those sounded particularly appropriate to him.

He decided to wander among the fiction section. There were some amazing authors there. He noted Sir Arthur Conan Doyle, H.G. Wells, and Charles Dickens among many others. It was a great collection. He couldn't see any modern fiction writers at all though. Nobody who had written anything in the last fifty years appeared on the shelves. He had only scoured the first two rooms, he reasoned though. There may well be a modern fiction section in the other rooms, and he had just not found it yet.

There was a table which had books and photographs of the town's history on it, and he headed towards it. In one of the photographs, he could see the main two streets in the center of the town, where the shops were. They were the same! Not just in the way the lay out and building structure, that wouldn't be that unusual. They were EXACTLY the same, with almost all of the same shops.

He could see Marion's sweet shop, the antiques shop, and the clothing shop, for example. He was sure Aubrey would give him some bullshit explanation about the shops being handed down through generations, if he were to ask her about it. Now that might be well be a valid explanation about one possibly, but all of them? No, that was impossible.

He picked up another picture. It was a picture of the town hall clock face. The clock was reading 3pm, exactly the time of his upcoming interview, he thought to himself, but he was prepared to concede that that must be just a coincidence. He didn't want to get paranoid. There were six or seven figures standing outside the town hall.

His eye was drawn to an exceptionally tall man in the middle of the portrait who dwarfed the other people. He must have been at least 6'7", Marcus thought. This man accentuated his height further, by wearing a top hat.

The woman standing next to him, in the photograph , was of particular interest. She wore a bonnet, which of course obscured her hair, but she had the same angular features and high cheekbones that Aubrey had... In fact, she looked exactly like Aubrey, in every way.

"Are you having fun?" Aubrey was behind him, clutching a couple of copies of his resume.

"Yes," Marcus replied, as blandly as he could manage. He was trying to hide his astonishment, at what he had just seen in the photos.

"I'm glad," she said. "I just want to pop in the special reserved section. I will only be a minute. Are you okay to carry on looking around for a bit?"

"Why don't I just come with you?" Said Marcus. "I haven't been in that room yet."

"I am sorry, but it is for family members only," she said. "You haven't got a card yet to prove you are one. When you do have a card, we can get you inside it."

"Ah, I understand, no worries." said Marcus.

"Don't worry," said Aubrey," I will be right back."

Evil In Ollenberry

With that, she glided over to the door to the special reserved section. Marcus strained to look through the door, as she opened it, but all he caught was a glimpse of what looked like very old leather-bound books on the shelves.

He wandered over to the desk. The librarian, an elderly lady with grey-blue and white permed hair, looked up from whatever she was reading, and smiled at him.

"Excuse me, he said. "I would like to get a library card."

"I know," said the lady smiling sweetly. "Aubrey told me you wanted one, and that you love books. You can get one next time you are here."

"Can I get one today?" Asked Marcus.

"No, not today," said the librarian. "Aubrey has put in the application. It has to be approved, and that shouldn't take long. Not in your case, I am sure."

"And who approves it, may I ask?" replied Marcus.

"The town council." said the librarian. "They approve all the important things."

"The town council approves the issuance of a library card? Is that right?" Marcus could not hide the fact that he felt incredulous at what she was telling him.

"Yes, absolutely," the librarian replied, her tone firm. "That's exactly what I am telling you." Then, she added, "I thought that Aubrey would have told you by now. We, in this town, value knowledge and family above all else."

"Yes, she told me that," Marcus replied.

"Well then," said the librarian, "now you understand."

"Yes," said Marcus. "I will get one next time. Thank you."

Marcus thought to himself, I don't understand, but there is no way I am going to argue the point with her. I am not going to get a library card today, whatever I say. And, arguing with the librarian will gain me nothing.

Aubrey had come out of the room by now. She had clearly taken some notes from whatever book or books she was looking at, as he saw her stuff a sheet of folded paper into her pocket.

"Did you get what you needed from the secret room?" said Marcus. He hadn't meant his voice to have any sarcasm to it, but he noticed that there was undoubtedly that tone to it.

"Why yes I did," said Aubrey full of enthusiasm. If she had noticed it, she had brushed it aside. "Now, let's get you up to see old man Tate."

Tate's was flat and square. A huge ugly 1970's style airport hangar, its functional design was in complete contrast to the lovely library, Marcus thought.

"You are not going to tell me that this is an old building too, are you, Aubrey? asked Marcus.

"Ha ha, of course not!" said Aubrey. "Most of it was built within the last fifty years, after a fire. The bit where Mr. Tate has his office, that's old. It managed to survive. He will probably call you in there. Just one thing before you go in. He likes to be called `Sir`, not Mr. Tate.   So, I suggest you go ahead and do that."

"Sure," said Marcus. "I will call Mr. Tate, `sir`."

"Thank you, babe," said Aubrey. "Good luck!"

Marcus walked up to the customer service desk. Manning the desk was a very bored looking, young woman with pink hair. Marcus informed her, that he was here to see Mr. Tate.

In response, she picked up the desk phone and mumbled something into it.

Her eyes widened slightly, in response to whatever she heard on the other end.

"He is ready to see you," said the young woman, "follow me please."

Marcus followed, as she swung sharply left, up a corridor and away from the neon lights of the hardware showroom. She opened a thick paneled, wooden door and entered another corridor. The ceiling became lower, so much so, that Marcus, at six feet, had to bend to go down the corridor.

The walls of the dim corridor were also wood paneled. Pictures were sparse and randomly scattered, all seemingly hung at crooked angles. Marcus could only get a glimpse of them as he passed, but they all seemed like individual portraits. The majority were women, but there were also men. As they approached another door, he noticed that there was an empty frame just by it. Somebody must be ready to hang another portrait there, he thought.

The young woman approached the door at the end of the corridor and knocked three times on it, without speaking.

"Mr. Tate will see you now. Go right on in." she said.

"Thank you," said Marcus, and he pushed the door open.

Evil In Ollenberry

The office inside was very dark. So dark in fact, that he could hardly see the figure behind the desk, whose face was in shadow.

"I am Mr. Tate. Please take a seat." The voice was deep and velvety, thought Marcus.

"Thank you, sir," said Marcus. "It's good to meet you." Marcus extended a hand, and Mr. Tate shook it, but remained seated. Marcus almost pulled back when they shook hands. Mr. Tate's was so cold, it felt like a corpse.

"Ah, I see you have brought some copies of your resume. Excellent. Please hand me one and wait in silence until I have read it."

"Yes sir," said Marcus.

It was impossible to see much detail in the room, beyond a few feet. The room was huge. Marcus noticed, that in the entirety of it, there was only one small lamp. The source of light was the desk lamp, which Mr. Tate was now using to read his resume.

The silence made Marcus feel uncomfortable, and he shivered as a reaction to the chill of the room. Thank goodness he was never going to really work for this guy, for any serious length of time, he thought. He was just going to play along with all of this weird shit, until he could escape. He had to try his best though, he reasoned. If he did anything to arouse their

Evil In Ollenberry

suspicion that he was planning to leave, there is no telling what the people in this creepy town would do.

Eventually, after what seemed like an interminable amount of time to Marcus, Mr. Tate spoke.

"I just have a few questions, Marcus," said Mr. Tate.

"Yes sir," said Marcus.

"We are a small community here, and customer care is very important to us. Do you think the customer is always right?" asked Mr. Tate.

"It's important that I do my best for the customer, whether he or she is right about something, or not. I need to do my best for them, so that they feel both respected and valued. That is what I will do, if I am selected to work for you." Marcus replied.

"Very good." said Mr. Tate. Then he added, "We have a really strong community ethic here, as I am sure you know by now, and we do require our employees to attend company functions. In fact, we are sponsoring the fancy dress party coming up soon, at which you are to be the guest of honor. Would you be able to attend our functions when we have them? All our staff love them, and we do pay everyone for attending. You would not have to go by yourself. You must bring Aubrey, of course."

"Yes, absolutely I would," Marcus replied, "and I am sure Aubrey would love to come too. She is very sociable."

Marcus could just about see that Mr. Tate was nodding approvingly.

"One last question, if I may," said Mr. Tate. "We have strong values here at Tate's. Do you have any idea what they might center around?"

"Family, loyalty and knowledge," Marcus replied

"Excellent!" exclaimed Mr. Tate. "You are hired! I know you have to give notice at your teaching job, but you can work all that out with our personnel department. I will see you soon."

"Thank you so much Sir, I am delighted", said Marcus," and Aubrey will be too."

"Good, I am very glad," said Mr. Tate.

"Are you okay showing yourself out? I have some paperwork I must complete, and I have to finish it by the close of business today. I hope you don't mind."

"I don't mind at all," said Marcus.

Marcus shut the door behind him, and after the gloom of Mr. Tate's office, he squinted at the lamplight in the corridor.

As soon as Marcus had left his office, Mr. Tate picked up his cellphone. "He's smart. Very smart. So, there's a chance, I agree with you. I have offered him a job. I still don't think he'll make it of course, but we will give it a whirl. If he doesn't work out though, we will have to accelerate the process. Time is running out, and we need one. We shall have to take risks.

We have to preserve our family and retain the knowledge. It is everything. Anyway, I take it you got what you needed from the library? I think he is still 'on board with things' shall we say, but better to make sure, just in case..." said Mr. Tate.

Marcus left Tate's and hurried over to where Aubrey was waiting for him.

"How did things go?" said Aubrey.

"It couldn't have gone better," Marcus replied. "I got the job! I will start at Tate's straight after my notice period on my teaching job. I will hand in my resignation tomorrow."

"Yayy! Congratulations!" said Aubrey excitedly. "I am so happy for you. So happy for us. And I have some more good news. Rusty, that local Bigfoot researcher, is going to meet us tomorrow at one of his favorite spots."

"Good, I don't have any classes tomorrow," Marcus replied," so we will have plenty of time to explore."

Now, it was just a question of waiting for the right opportunity, thought Marcus. While Aubrey was in the bathroom, he prepared a small grab and go bag which included his passport, a few family mementos, as well as a change of clothes. He buried it at the back of the closet, hiding it behind a small pile of his clothes. Clothes that he knew Aubrey was not fond of. He would go tonight if he could. He was sorry to leave his stuff behind, but better that... than dead.

He waited to see if Aubrey would go into a deep sleep and start snoring. She remained silent though. He felt like she was waiting for something too, and that disturbed him. He had to try though. He tried to slip out of the bedroom as silently as he could, and headed for the kitchen.

"Babe, are you okay?" said Aubrey, almost as soon as he had left.

"Yes, I am fine, don't worry," he replied. "I was just a little hungry, that's all. I will be back with you in a minute."

"Good," she said, "because I am already missing you."

"I am missing you too," Marcus replied. "I will be just a minute."

There was no chance of an escape tonight, he thought. I will just have to wait for another opportunity.

As he lay next to her, not sleeping, he weighed up his options. There would be a time he could go soon, there must be. He messaged both Ed and his sister, to say he was fine. There was undoubtedly some sort of paranormal phenomenon to this business, no matter how reluctant he was to admit it. He would call his friend David to see what he could pick up. David was a very gifted psychic, and they had been friends for years. If anyone could give him any insight into these people, then it was him.

He wished he had thought of that a few days ago, but everything had been so intense and overwhelming. On a positive note, if they were getting him a job and inviting him to parties, then maybe they weren't trying to kill him after all. Aubrey had been very sweet to him, he couldn't deny that. What did they want with him then? He had no idea how he could fit into their plans. He wasn't going to hang around to find out though, that was for certain.

Eventually, he fell asleep, and by the time he woke up, Aubrey was already awake and dressed. She informed him that Rusty had sent them the rendezvous coordinates, and they were to meet him there at 11 a.m. sharp.

"I was just going to wake you babe," said Aubrey. "Boy, did you sleep good."

"Yes," he replied. "I must have needed it, what with all the excitement over the last few days and all."

"You have had a busy time, that's certainly true," Aubrey replied. "Nobody could blame you for needing some extra rest. Are you good with grabbing a quick coffee from Pete's before we meet up with Rusty? It's on the way."

"Absolutely," Marcus replied.

"Hey! Here he is! The great bear hunter! Quite the talk of the town, you are," said Pete jovially, when they arrived at his little coffee hut.

"He's had a rough time," said Aubrey, with a touch of disapproval in her voice.

"I know, I completely understand," Pete replied. "I am just messing with you. I am seriously impressed. Here have these two coffees on me."

"Thank you so much," said Marcus.

"No problem at all," Pete replied. "I will see you soon."

Marcus and Aubrey arrived almost exactly on time at the research spot. Two men were waiting for them in a red jeep. They waved, and then proceeded to walk over to them after Aubrey had parked.

Marcus jumped out and strode over to them. Aubrey was always quick out of the vehicle, but this time he noticed that she was trailing behind a little for some reason.

"Hey good to meet you," said the smaller and older of the two men, "I am Rusty, and this is my son Wes."

"It's good to see you," Marcus replied, shaking hands with them both as he did so. "Thanks so much for agreeing to show us your research area." Marcus said." Aubrey and I are very grateful."

Aubrey had bounded over by now, a beaming smile on her face. "Good to meet you,"she said shaking hands with Rusty. He returned the smile.

When she shook hands with Wes though, the latter quickly drew back. Marcus could see that Wes was unmistakably frowning at her. Did the two of them know each other? Marcus didn't think so. So, what had caused such thinly veiled hostility in Wes when he shook hands with her. Aubrey seemed a bit startled by his reaction, and she seemed to share the same dislike. She wiped her hands down her trousers, the moment she broke off her handshake with Wes. She quickly regained her composure, smiling again at Rusty.

Wes on the other hand, looked straight at Aubrey, staring, before his eyes flicked over to

Marcus. Marcus felt the scrutiny. Wes had sensed something and showed a visible dislike of Aubrey the moment they made physical contact. They were not part of this town. Wes and Rusty could be allies, Marcus thought, and help him escape. They only lived about an hour away.

"Welcome to my research area," Rusty began. "I hope you enjoy it. Please, come over here," he said, pulling a map from his pocket, before opening it out on the hood of the jeep. "This forest is eleven miles long, by two miles wide. As you can see this area connects with forests and woodland over a hundred miles wide, across the whole of southern Ohio. The epicenter of Bigfoot activity is here though. Right in this forest. I suggest that you focus your research right here," he said, pointing to a dot on the map, about three miles from where they were parked.

"We have brought a couple of trail cams with us,"said Marcus, "and a sound recording device, so we can certainly deploy them and get started today."

"That's great," Rusty replied. Then he added, "You have to be careful though, the bigfoot's here can be very hostile."

"Hostile?" said Marcus, "what do you mean?"

"I mean they seem to take a particular dislike to some people, and we don't know why," Rusty explained. "For example, there was a local couple who were camping here by an old, abandoned cabin. They had pitched up their tent by it and placed their provisions in it. In the middle of the night, they heard a commotion in the cabin. When they went to investigate it, they saw two enormous creatures, one of which they described as being black, and the other white, tearing it up. They instantly fled and never returned."

"There are also incidents of people having sticks and rocks thrown at them, for no apparent reason. Just last month, a couple were out hiking here, when `something` threw sticks at them, one of which caused the woman's face to be gashed so badly that she had to have multiple stiches in hospital. They filed an official report," said Rusty.

"What has been causing them to behave like this? Do you know?"asked Marcus.

"We really don't have any idea," Rusty replied. "Nowhere else in this area has the same concentration of aggressive activity. There are some other incidents sure, particularly around the Dragon's mound, but nothing like we have here."

"What is the Dragon's mound?" asked Marcus.

"It's an ancient archaeological site," said Wes, interjecting. "There are all sorts of theories on who built it, and when. All we know for sure though, is that it was built by an ancient people many thousands of years ago."

Marcus noted that that he was staring directly at Aubrey as he spoke. Aubrey meanwhile was looking at the ground, looking almost sheepish.

"Yes, and there is a lot of paranormal activity here," said Rusty. There is an old graveyard just down the road. People have reported seeing spirits there, particularly the ghost of an old lady."

"That is something I would like to investigate at another time", said Marcus.

"I agree, you should certainly go there at some point in the future," said Rusty. "In terms of paranormal activity here, a lot of it centers around what archaeologists think is an ancient, abandoned fort, built on a hilltop, which is a couple of miles from here. The old cabin, where the couple saw the two bigfoots, is at the midpoint of the woods, about five miles from here."

"I think there is enough daylight for us to make both of them and get back, if we hurry," said Marcus. "What do you think, Aubrey?"

"I think that's a great idea," she replied." Why don't we go straightaway? We will really have to move it if we are going to do them both and set up the trail cameras."

Marcus noticed that Aubrey was so anxious to leave, that she was starting to move towards the trail.

"Is there anything else you need to tell us for now," said Marcus?

"I don't think so," said Rusty. "Just please be careful. Let me know when you get out of the woods as well. Remember, you can't get a phone signal until you get a mile away from where our vehicles are parked. As soon as you get off the dirt track though, you should be able to pick one up."

"That's great," said Marcus, "I will certainly call you later."

Aubrey was now already twenty yards or so up the trail, walking slowly. She turned and waved, shouting a goodbye, before she carried on.

"She is keen on getting started," said Marcus, who was feeling a little embarrassed that Aubrey had already turned to leave.

"She is certainly that," Wes replied. "Look, I have your phone number off Rusty. He was scribbling on a piece of paper as he talked. Here is mine, just in case Rusty isn't available, and you need me in an emergency."

Marcus didn't know whether he could trust the two of them just yet, or whether this was another kind of `game` of Aubrey's. The reaction of Wes towards Aubrey, the evident hostility, and in turn her reaction to it, certainly gave him hope. They were nearby, and could prove to be very useful to his escape.

"Rusty, I will certainly give you a quick call tonight. I would like to call both of you, to talk about the mythology of the area, and any potential Bigfoot activity, if that's okay,"said Marcus.

"That's a good idea," said Rusty. "I am not as young as I used to be, and my boy Wes has been to quite a few new places recently."

Marcus hurried down the trail, trying to catch Aubrey, who had now disappeared.

He looked around for her, but she was nowhere to be seen.

"Boo!" She said, jumping out behind him, and laughing as she   did so.

"Wow, I have never seen you so keen to get going," he remarked.

"Uh, I'm sorry Babe," said Aubrey," I just really didn't like those guys at all."

"Why not?" said Marcus.

"I just think that they were really sexist," she replied. "Especially that guy Wes. I felt he was hostile towards me, just because I was a woman. I really think that no matter what I said, he would disapprove of it."

"I didn't pick up on any sexism from either of them, I am surprised you thought that", Marcus replied.

"That's because you are not a woman," said Aubrey, before heading off up the trail again. This time a lot more rapidly.

The gradient was steep, yet Aubrey never got tired, stopping occasionally to look at the odd flower, or insect that was of interest to her. Marcus did the same, although he had to concede that it required much more effort for him, than it did for Aubrey.

She was strong and fit. He thought. Not just strong and fit when compared to an average middle-aged woman, or even an athlete. Her strength was supernatural. It was really incredible.

He wondered if he might be able to lose her here. In these woods. He could walk out, and call Wes and Rusty. Whether they believed his story or not, all they had to do was drop him off in the next town. He could wait there for Ed.

She might come looking for him though, checking hotels for example. She knew he had no car. So, he would have to take a cab to somewhere much farther away. He would try it here. He was going to just pick a moment to run.

Evil In Ollenberry

The climb continued for about forty minutes, before finally levelling out into a plateau. The area was beautiful. The ancient forest here was bisected by a beautiful creek, which seemed to glisten as it wound gently through it. There were also butterflies. Butterflies everywhere he looked. They danced and swirled all around him. They were seemingly rising on the beams of light, which had penetrated the verdant canopy above.

"What a breathtakingly beautiful place," said Marcus.

"It is," said Aubrey, rather blandly. Still, she loved dancing, and she began doing just that. She began twirling through the light beams, with the butterflies, as she moved up the trail.

After only a few minutes, they came to what must be the abandoned fort, Marcus reckoned. To the right of the trail, a steep hill rose about three hundred feet into the air. It was impossible to see the top of it, from where they stood on the trail, as it was covered in trees. The feature was unmistakable though.

"I think I would like to go up this hill, and set at least one of the trail cameras up there, if that's okay with you," said Marcus.

"Sure," Aubrey replied. "Where were you thinking of putting the other one?"

"Probably somewhere near the cabin. Then we can walk back before we lose the light." Marcus replied.

"That sounds good," said Aubrey.

Marcus thought that he could lose Aubrey in the fading light. He had no problem being in the forest at night, and he reckoned that was his best chance.

"Let's get up there then," said Marcus, before turning off the trail, and heading into the thick vegetation beyond it. Aubrey joined him, skipping right by his side.

As soon as he got off the trail, Marcus felt it. A thickness in the air. The hill wasn't a long climb, but now he felt like he was back in Nepal, trekking through the mountains. He looked to his side. Even Aubrey was now struggling. He saw that her head was down, and that she was breathing heavily.

What is going on here, he thought to himself. It's like the oxygen has almost totally disappeared.

"I am not sure we should carry on," said Aubrey. "Something feels wrong." Marcus sensed fear in her voice.

For her to say that, Marcus thought, there must be something very wrong indeed. Yet, maybe wrong for her, was good for him. Maybe this was the time he could get away? He had never seen her afraid before. His chances to escape could be few, where she was concerned.

Given her unnatural physical capacities, he was unsure whether he could lose her on the trail, even in the dark. Here though, he had the advantage. He was finding it tough, but she was barely able to forge up the hill. Now might be his chance.

"I think I am going to have to stop," said Aubrey. She was panting hard. "I don't know what is wrong with me,"she said.

"It's only another fifty yards or so to the top. Are you sure?" said Marcus.

"Absolutely," said Aubrey. "The further I go towards the top, the worse I feel. You go on up there, and I will wait here."

Marcus sensed his chance. "Okay then, I will just set up one of the trail cameras and be right down."

As soon as he pulled away from her, the remaining part of the climb became much easier. He decided to set up a trail camera. If she did struggle to the top he reasoned, and she found that there was not one there, she would know straight away that he had been lying to her.

On the other hand, if he put one up, she would waste time in the surrounding area, looking for him. That might well give him the time he needed to get away, running as fast as he could down the trail.

He found a great place to set one, and he carefully strapped it to a tree. The location had full visibility of both the peak of the abandoned fort, and the downslope that led up to it.

Now, Marcus decided, it was time to run!

Then he heard her scream. It wasn't a scream of frustration. Marcus had heard Aubrey scream like that before. It was one of terror, a guttural scream, and so high pitched and resonant that his first instinct was to cover his ears. Was it a trick, or was she really in some sort of mortal danger?

He had just moments to decide what to do. He couldn't in good conscience leave her there. Whatever she was or was not doing, it would haunt him for the rest of his life. He knew that was a fact. So, he turned, and flew down the slope.

He could see that Aubrey was crouched down, with her hands covering her head. Then he saw a stick fly through the air, and bounce right off the top of her head. She staggered, before falling onto her hands and knees.

"Aubrey! Aubrey!" He shouted.

Evil In Ollenberry

"Help me babe!" She whimpered. "They are attacking me!"

Who were they? He thought. He spun around, but he could see nothing. A rock flew straight past him, causing him to dart to the side. He followed the direction, from which it was thrown from.

Then he saw it. Just a flash, but that flash was enough to amaze him. A huge black arm shot quickly back into the foliage. It was no bear! The creature he saw, had a huge gorilla-like hand!

It's a Bigfoot! A damn bigfoot is attacking her! This place is insane, he thought.

By now he had reached her. He quickly got to his feet. His peripheral vison caught another creature! This one was white, running rapidly, before launching a stone straight at them. He ducked as it flew over his head.

Aubrey had a livid and bloody gash across her cheek. She stuttered as she said, "The creatures! They attacked. We need to get out of here!"

Three grunts, and then a huge bellowing roar came from the top of the hill.

"More of them are on the way! she exclaimed, the horror showing in her eyes.

"Yes," Marcus replied. "I think these two are flanking us, not yet feeling emboldened to attack us directly. I would imagine though that when those others come, they certainly will!"

He pulled Aubrey down the hill, pushing her on as fast as he could, doing his best to shield her from the missiles. A large stick hit his back, which caused him to stagger. Somehow, he maintained his footing. He knew that if he fell now, they were both done for.

They jumped in unison onto the trail. The moment they did so, Aubrey seemed to regain her strength.

"Let's run," she said, "before the others come!"

Marcus didn't need to be persuaded. They had some ground on the creatures, they were waiting for reinforcements, so they had a chance. He bounded down the trail after Aubrey, who was sprinting so quickly that he could already hardly see her.

Sweat now began to blur his vision. He thought he saw one run past his right-hand side, through the trees. Then another one ran past him, on his left side. Maybe it was the white one, he thought. They were going to be able to cut him off. With the other Bigfoots coming up behind, he would be trapped.

He had to carry on running though, he had no alternative. Even, if it was to his death.

He waited to be smashed into at any moment, but to his amazement, it did not happen. Now, he could see the car. Aubrey was inside it and driving towards him. A stick bounced off the car's hood, as she sped towards him.

"Jump in!" She said. Marcus threw himself into the car, just as a huge rock smashed into the ground beside the car's right tire.

Aubrey pushed the car into a shuddering reverse, before turning and roaring the car down the dirt track.

"Those bastards," she said. "Let's see if they can catch us in this!" The moment she spoke, the car began to stutter.

Instinctively, Marcus turned around. He turned just in time, to see two huge creatures running up the hill towards the car. One white, one black. They were both massive.

The white one he estimated, must be at least seven feet tall, while the black one must be a little under. Both had pointed heads, and huge muscular physiques. They looked much more powerful than a gorilla , Marcus thought, and he had seen silverback gorillas in the wild.

"They are coming!" Marcus shouted, frustration, as the car's speed dropped drastically.

The car was now barely moving forward, at fifteen miles an hour.

"They are using intentional magic," said Aubrey.

"I don't understand?" Marcus replied.

"I don't have time to explain all of it," said Aubrey. "Basically though, it's about manifesting desires. They are imagining the car breaking down, and it IS breaking down! We must do the opposite."

"What?" said Marcus.

"Trust me," said Aubrey." Close your eyes and imagine the car speeding up, getting us out of here. Do it now."

There was no time to debate it, Marcus knew that, so he closed his eyes and imagined the car going faster. He imagined it speeding out of here, as though they were on a freeway rather than a dirt track.

At first, the engine coughed like an old man with bronchitis. Then the car suddenly lurched forward, before it began gaining speed.

"We did it!" Aubrey shouted triumphantly. "We are leaving them behind!"

Marcus turned to see the two creatures had given up the chase. The white one stood with its arm around the smaller, black one. The hairy black creature, was holding it's head in its hands. Disturbingly, the smaller one appeared to be weeping. He wasn't sure though. In that moment, he was just glad to be alive.

"I have been waiting all my life to see a Bigfoot," said Marcus. "When I finally do, not one, but two of them attack me! I have never seen anything even remotely like this. We need to get your face taken care of at the hospital, and then I should call Rusty."

"There is an old-time healing woman only ten minutes drive from here, we can go to her," said Aubrey.

"You need a hospital and some stitches," said Marcus. "Not the `healing woman`, " said Marcus. "You need a professional to help you!"

"We are going to the damned healing woman!" snapped Aubrey.

They spent the last few minutes of the journey in silence, before Aubrey pulled up at a small brown shack with a covered porch.

A seemingly ancient looking woman sat on it, rocking in her chair. She had a brown shawl draped across her paper-thin body.

"You wait here." said Aubrey sternly.

Marcus didn't reply. Aubrey spoke to the woman, but Marcus could hear that it was in that strange local language that he did not understand. The woman didn't respond with any conversation of her own. She merely nodded, and beckoned Aubrey inside, opening the door of the shack as she did so. Aubrey entered the place, and the door to the shack slammed shut.

Marcus briefly considered making a run for it, but he quickly dismissed the idea. He was exhausted. He couldn't have gone far, he knew that. Plus, now the adrenaline had gone, his back hurt like hell.

He was shocked when Aubrey came out of the shack smiling, with the healing woman trailing behind. The cut on her cheek was almost completely healed!

"That wound should have needed at least ten stiches, how did she manage that?" Marcus was shocked.

"I told you she was good," said Aubrey, winking at him.

"There is good, and there is miraculous!" said Marcus. "That wound should have taken weeks to heal, and yet there it is, barely noticeable. That's remarkable."

Aubrey ignored the question. "Elsie says that you are injured too. You have hurt your back apparently? I am really sorry, babe. Please go with her though, she can heal you."

"Okay," said Marcus. "After what she did for you, I am willing to give anything a shot."

"Great, thank you," said Aubrey. "I will wait for you outside."

Elsie the healing woman, looked at him impassively, beckoning him into the shack, by opening the door.

As soon as he got to his feet, Marcus felt the fatigue in his body, and he hobbled to the door.

The inside of the shack was sparsely furnished. An old-fashioned wood burning stove stood in the far corner of the small, one room structure. A crooked iron frame bed, a small table and two wood, straight back chairs were in the corner opposite the stove.

The air inside the shack was almost insufferably hot and smoky. There were unfinished wood shelves, covering the the almost entirety of the walls, on which sat rows of labelled glass jars.

Elsie didn't speak, she merely motioned him to lie down on the bed, which he duly complied with, taking off his shirt as he did so.

He turned his face to the right, and saw the healer grab a rag, and pour some liquid onto it form one of the bottles. Then, she grabbed a huge bone which was resting on the table, the like of which Marcus had never seen before.

Marcus felt her rub the rag onto his back. The pressure was painful and cold, and it made him wince. Then, he heard the old woman mumble something. Then, she pressed the bone hard into his back, with more strength than he could have imagined she had.

In contrast to the liquid, the bone felt hot. He felt warmth and energy shoot into his body. Almost immediately he felt energized! It was as if the events of the last few hours had never happened. He jumped off the bed.

"Thank you." said Marcus.

"Kawenkal", said Elsie, in response.

"I have no idea what that means, but I am very grateful," said Marcus.

CHAPTER FOUR

-You Are Going Nowhere-

"I thought they were all dead in this area, and that only a few were left up at snake mound." said Aubrey.

"I thought so too," said the voice on the other end of the phone line, "but nonetheless you shouldn't have gone there. You should have pretended you had an injury on the trail, before you got to the fort."

"I agree. I was complacent, but it is done now. On a positive note," Aubrey added, "Marcus did well. I have to give him credit for saving me."

"Yes, he was very impressive from what you have told me," said the voice. Maybe he is the one we have been looking for. I am actually looking forward to the next trial."

"I think he may be suspicious though. I sense that he is masking something from me," said Aubrey. "In any event, we can't let him talk to anyone about what happened today."

"Then you know what you need to do tonight," said the voice. "You can't wait."

"I know," said Aubrey. "She looked and saw Marcus approaching the car. "He's coming out now. I have to go."

"How are you feeling, babe?" said Aubrey.

"I feel amazing," said Marcus. "I can't believe what you she did. She got some liquid out, and a strange giant bone. Rubbed it on me, and then I felt better than I have in years! I have to call Rusty and Wes! They are going to be amazed."

"Don't worry about them," said Aubrey "I just called Rusty. I told him that we had tough time in the woods, and that you were exhausted. I explained that you needed to rest, and that you would call him in the morning."

"A tough time! What happened was absolutely sensational!" Marcus replied.

"Yes, it was," said Aubrey, then she added. "I am sure you realize by now, that when it comes to healing, Elsie knows best. She said that we both need to go to bed and sleep when we get home."

"Okay," said Marcus, "I can't deny that Elsie is a miracle worker. I will do as she asks."

"Thank you," Babe,"You saved me. You are amazing." said Aubrey. "I am sorry I was so grumpy earlier. I was just so stressed. I thought I might die."

"Not at all," Marcus replied. "I totally understand. What we both went through was astounding! Those creatures that attacked us... They were both impressive and terrifying at the same time! We were actually attacked by a group of Bigfoots! And, then that magic to get the car going! I am struggling to process it all."

"That's another reason why we must get back," said Aubrey "It's not just our bodies that need resting, our mind's need it too."

Aubrey nearly always took a long time to go to sleep, and waiting for her to do so had been difficult for Marcus. After each day's events, he had normally been exhausted. Not so tonight though.

The healing woman had not just healed him. Whatever she had done, had also had left him completely refreshed. He hoped it hadn't affected Aubrey to the same degree though. She seemed tired as they went to bed this time though, and he was pleasantly surprised at how quick she started snoring.

Still, he waited. It was an hour before he slipped out of bed, grabbed his little bag and slipped quietly out of the bedroom.

Slowly, he opened the front door, and crept out into the night. His heart was beating quickly. Once outside, he paused for just a moment to listen. He could hear no movement from inside the house, and he could even hear Aubrey snoring. Wonderful!

The most difficult part of the plan had been executed! He thought to himself.

He had decided that he would keep walking throughout the night, and when it became daylight, he would find a place to hide for the day. Then, he would wait for darkness to fall again, before he continued walking. He would only travel under the cover of the night.

He had enough food and water to adequately sustain him for a couple of nights, when he imagined the search for him would be at it's most intense.

After that, he would contact Ed from whatever small town he had made it to by then. He had no idea where it would be, that depended on the amount of traffic. He would have to hide from any cars that were on the road. There shouldn't be too many though, in this middle of nowhere place.

The farther he got, the better chance he had of escaping. Even Aubrey and the Ollensberry townsfolk had limited resources. There were only so many of them, after all.

He headed toward the far end of the garden. As he did so, he heard something big run down the road, behind the tree line and on towards the end of the garden. A coyote maybe? It certainly sounded bigger than that, but he couldn't afford to worry about it.

He was on his way. He got to the fence that marked the edge of the property and began climbing over it. His foot hit hard against something. He wasn't sure what it was? It was almost like he was bashing against glass, but that was impossible!

He turned and attempted to jump down off the fence, but found that he couldn't. Instead, he just slammed hard into whatever was behind the fence. Confused, he climbed back down. What was going on? He thought?

Now, he reached above the fence, and pressed. There was a wall, there was no doubt about it. An invisible barrier! He ran all around that side of the garden, pressing above the fence as he did so. There was solid, invisible wall around the garden fence.

He ran towards the opposite side of Aubrey's property, towards Ollenberry. He reckoned he could make it through the town and into the countryside beyond if he ran part of the way.

Again though, he hit the barrier. In frustration, he banged his head against it. He was trapped! Then, he realized he had a chance. The barrier mustn't stretch across the road. It had to let cars through. He would wait until one went past, and then jump through whatever breach in the barrier it created.

It was twenty minutes before one finally came through, and by then Marcus was fraught. He crouched down by the side of the road, waiting until the car drew parallel to him, then he jumped straight into the place where it had just driven from.

Bouncing straight off the barrier, his head hit the road with a smack, and pain shot through his body. He groaned with the pain and curled up into a ball.

"What are you trying to do, Babe, are you trying to get another trip to the healing woman? The old barrier there, it's just for you. Nice try, but of course cars can pass through it," said Aubrey.

Marcus hauled himself to his feet. He could see a dark patch on the floor in the moonlight It must be his own blood, but he could not feel where he was bleeding from.

"You can't keep me here," he shouted at Aubrey, defiantly.

"I can do what I want, babe," said Aubrey. "And I am keeping you here. Why? Because **that's** what I want."

"For what purpose though?" said Marcus. "I don't understand."

"You don't need to understand. You are just going to play the game. You are smart. There's just a chance you could win."

"There is not a chance in hell that I am going to play any more of these crazy games," Marcus shouted." I can promise you that!"

"Yes, you will," said Aubrey. "You are going to forget now. And then we will be happy again."

She waved her hand, and as she did so, Marcus saw a red and orange ball begin to glow, forming at her fingertips. He ducked, as it flew towards him, and it whizzed straight over his head.

Aubrey laughed at this. "Tricky," She said, "but you can't win."

Instinctively, Marcus spun around to face the ball, which was now as big as his head. It hovered in the air above him, as if waiting for a command. He didn't see the one that slammed into his back. He just felt it, cold like a ball of ice, pushing through his skin, and punching straight into his brain.

Aubrey caught him as he started falling to the ground.

"Goodnight, babe." she said.

CHAPTER FIVE

-Elsie-

Marcus opened his eyes. That chase they had endured, with the bears, must have taken more out of him than he had first imagined. Maybe he had had an adrenaline crash, or the healing woman had put him to sleep in some way, he couldn't remember. Yet he had woken up on her bed.

Evil In Ollenberry

"Hello?" He called out. There was no reply. He got up and looked around the shack. There was nobody there. He opened the door and went outside. Aubrey and Elsie were outside. The latter was still wrapped in her shawl, rocking in her chair.

"Yawarl dina combustula" He heard Aubrey say to Elsie.

"Gransita," Elsie replied, with a smile.

"Wow babe," said Aubrey turning to face him as she did so. "You really needed a rest. That chase with the bears has really wiped you out. You must have really needed that rest."

"I guess so," Marcus said. "And the bears, I remember going to the Fort, and them chasing us, but that's all I remember. Are you okay?" He asked.

"Yes," I am good she replied. "Elsie took care of me. And I have good news about the bears. It turns out some rich idiot had been keeping them in a private zoo. He had probably been mistreating them, that's why they behaved so badly. Anyway, today they were caught and euthanized. You won't have to worry about the bears again."

"I am sorry that the bears were euthanized," Marcus replied, "but I guess the authorities had no choice. "They would have undoubtedly killed someone if they hadn't been stopped."

"Yes, I agree. It's all over the local news as well," said Aubrey. "And you saved me!" She added. "One had come hurtling towards me, and you pushed me out of the way. You were quite the hero yesterday. You were amazing! I love you so much!"

Aubrey grabbed his face in both her hands, before kissing him softly on the lips.

Marcus felt confused. He remembered the bears of course. He didn't remember pushing Aubrey out of the way, but it had all happened so fast.

"I called Rusty and told him the story. He said that he was horrified, of course. He told you to rest, and that he will speak to you in a few days." said Aubrey.

"Okay great. I don't have any classes until tomorrow, they are my penultimate one's." he said.

"That works out just fine. I have to go and get some fancy-dress costumes for the kids today, so I will be busy doing that. You can just stay and chill at the house, if that's okay?" she said.

"I have no problem doing that," said Marcus.

He fell asleep almost as soon as he got back to the house. When he awoke, it was getting dark. As Aubrey was not in the house, he decided to check his phone. There were no calls from her, but there were three missed calls from his friend Ed. I wonder why he was so persistent. Marcus thought.

He grabbed a coffee and gave him a call.

"Hey, how are you doing?" asked Marcus. "I saw you tried to call me a few times today, I am sorry I had a really rough time with some bears. I needed to sleep. I have just woken up."

"Bears again?" said Ed. "What is going on in that town!"

"It turns out that some idiot had a couple locked up in a private zoo. It seems he was mistreating them." Marcus said.

"Uh huh." said Ed. He sounded suspicious, which surprised Marcus.

"I didn't phone you about the bears," said Ed. "My private detective friend did some digging on that Simon Cornish guy."

"I don't remember any Simon Cornish guy," said Marcus, sounding puzzled.

"Yes, you do!" said Ed, the frustration evident in his voice. "He was the guy whose paper you found outside the fire, after the family had been burning them and reciting some strange language. Do you remember, **that**," said Ed?

"Vaguely," said Marcus. "Some silly game the kids were playing, I think."

"You thought it was much more than just a silly game, last time we spoke," said Ed, "but I didn't call you to argue with you. That guy, Simon Cornish, has just disappeared! This was only a month or so ago. He said he was visiting a girlfriend in Ohio, and then boom!" He is gone.

Marcus frowned. He felt a sharp pain, suddenly shoot into his head, like it was being pierced by an arrow. Then he replied, "t must be just a coincidence," he said.

"Just a coincidence? Are you kidding me!" Ed exclaimed. "That town is creepy as shit! Something bad is going down there, I am telling you! I am damn well coming to get you. It's going to take me a few days, as I am right on the opposite side of the country, but I am coming!"

"There is really no need," said Marcus. "I am completely fine and really happy. I am so happy."

There was a pause on the other end of the phone. Now Ed spoke softly and slowly, "of course you are buddy. I will just come for a visit, okay? I would just like to see you."

Evil In Ollenberry

"We can just phone one another, I am good. I don't want to put you to any trouble." Marcus replied.

"I am sorry, I am losing the signal," said Ed. Then he was gone.

Marcus tried to ring him back, but Ed's phone went straight to voicemail. Ed was being a bit paranoid, Marcus thought. There was nothing wrong with his life here. He was doing really well.

It wasn't long before Aubrey got back home.

"What fancy dress costumes did you get?" Marcus replied.

"Ah, it's a surprise," said Aubrey." I can't wait to show you them though, but it isn't long until the party."

"I got some take out," said Aubrey. "I know you have been resting today, but are you good with that and an early night?"

"Yes, I could do with that. I have to teach tomorrow, and it's only a few days until I start at Tate's. So, I am happy to get as much rest as I possibly can."

Marcus didn't get up that night. He slept so soundly, that he didn't hear the angry roar which came from outside. Just past the edge of Aubrey's property...

Over summer, Marcus's school was quiet. From September until May, the main term, he would teach about nineteen students, but during summer, the numbers were low.

Goodbyes had always made Marcus feel awkward, so only having these last three students to say goodbye to, made him feel much better. He had become very fond of the one's that were left. Max, from Germany, Cindy from Switzerland, and Adam from France. They were all exceedingly smart, and all of them were at the end of their advanced English courses. Max and Adam were both due to enter their family businesses soon. Cindy was highly technical and was due to go into computer programing.

The last two lessons were around business terminology. Marcus was a planner, and had the lessons prepared almost perfectly. They were a good group to end on, he thought. They were all punctual and inquisitive. He took the classes via Zoom in Aubrey's little study. The only time he ever came in here was to conduct the lessons. For some reason, he had always found the room to be very cold, even in the baking heat of an Ohio summer. The room was also a bit creepy, he thought.

On the wall a black canopy had been draped, which covered Aubrey's clothes. It contained Zodiac signs and mystical symbols, which Aubrey had told him she had made herself. That didn't particularly bother him.

What was of most concern to him were the collection of what Aubrey described as `haunted objects` that she had. Some she had locked away, these included a clown called Banjo, whom, she said, would cause trouble whenever he could. There was also a picture of a man in a pinstripe suit. The man, she said, was particularly dangerous. According to Aubrey, he would seek to break out of the picture whenever he could, and Aubrey would have to bind him into it. The one she left out was a small china doll, which she had called Beth.

Beth, she said, had sweet energy around her. Marcus couldn't argue that she wasn't less sinister than the other two. She certainly looked harmless, with pigtails. A flowery dress and accentuated blue eyes. His students had seen the doll and the canopy when he had first started using Zoom from the office, and he had told them their background. They were all young people, in their late teens and early twenties, and they had enjoyed teasing him about them for a few minutes, before focusing back on the lesson. He had laughed along too, but at the same time, he would not be sorry when he left the room.

As expected, all his students were on time. After brief hello's, they got straight down to business. Marcus had a lot to go through in this lesson, to wrap up the course before he left.

He was busy explaining the context and nature of what a patent is, when Max interrupted him.

"I am sorry Marcus, but there is a lot of buzzing at your end, can you turn it down please?"

Marcus was a little puzzled, but technical glitches were nothing new to online teaching.

"I am sorry Max," Marcus replied. "Can you all hear the buzzing?"

"I can," said Adam. "Me too," replied Cindy. "It is getting stronger. And there is something else."

"What is it?" Marcus replied.

Cindy stared at him, blinking hard as she did so. "Oh, it's nothing. It has stopped now, don't worry about it."

Adam added, "yes the buzzing seems to be dying down too, I –"

He suddenly cut off what he was saying, in mid-sentence. At first, Marcus thought he might be thinking of the correct terminology in English. This had been a hard lesson after all, and they were right at the end of it. Then he saw that Adam was focused entirely on the screen. In fact, all three of them were staring intently at it.

"Are you guys all okay?" Said Marcus. "You have all gone very quiet. Can I help you with anything?"

"No, I am good," said Max. "Me too," replied Cindy. "And me" replied Max.

"Okay then," said Marcus. 'Well, we are about finished now. Let's come back tomorrow for our final lesson. I hope you all enjoy the Los Angeles sunshine for the rest of the day."

The students said their goodbyes, and he switched off the Zoom. Silently, he stepped out of the room. He always felt like he had to hold his breath when he came out of it.

What had been going on with his students today? Glitches were one thing, but they had behaved very differently from normal when that happens. If the internet was starting to get troublesome out here in the country, then he was glad he was starting at Tate's in a few days.

His phone was ringing. It was David, his psychic friend from Scotland. Marcus had forgotten that he had arranged to speak to him straight after his lesson today, but he was glad of the distraction.

"How are you, David?" He said.

"I am good," David replied, "I have been worried about you though, how are things going?"

"You don't need to worry about me. I am doing really well."

"Has anything odd happened since you got there?" said David.

"There was this weird problem with these bears," said Marcus." A couple escaped from a private zoo that this idiot was running. I was extremely unlucky with them, or lucky if you consider that I survived my tangle with them. Apart from that I am good though."

"Bears? said David, sounding alarmed." I heard nothing about it."

"I am surprised you didn't. It was all over the local news here." Marcus replied.

"I will check it out," said David." I am sure I can find something about it on the Internet."

"What about Aubrey?" David asked. "I really care about how you are. It was always a risk to go there, you knew that."

"I know you care," Marcus replied defensively, "and I really appreciate it. I couldn't be happier. Aubrey and her family have all been very good to me."

"I am very glad about that," said David, but you know how I am. "I always blunt with you. And I sense something wrong. Not just that, but every time I try to focus on you, I feel a pain behind my eyes, and a kind of fuzziness. I can't explain it, except to say that it feels like some kind of psychic block."

Marcus had been prepared to politely dismiss his friend's concerns, until he said that. For the fuzziness and pain were exactly the same symptoms he had been feeling since the bear attack.

"Can you read Aubrey," Marcus said?

"She is very strange to read," he replied. "It's like she has some sort of veil up. I didn't try to push through it, but I will, if I have your permission to do so,"said David.

"Yes, absolutely," said Marcus. "You have my permission to do whatever it takes."

The moment he said this, Marcus felt the same fuzzy feeling, the same pain. "You have it right now, don't you?" said David.

"Yes, I do," said Marcus. Clutching the side of his head as he spoke.

"Look, let's talk again in the next few days," said David. "I seem to do better trying to reach you at night for some reason." I will try over the next few nights. And then get back to you, if that's okay?"

"Yes please," said Marcus." My last school lesson is tomorrow, but I don't start that new position as Tate's, the local department store here for a few days, so I have plenty of time."

Almost immediately after he had finished talking to David, the phone rang. It was his sister. Marcus decided to ignore the call, which made him feel better. The fuzziness began to clear, and the horrendous headache he had, almost completely disappeared.

It was as if it was associated with Aubrey, he considered. Good thoughts about her meant that he felt strong. Bad thoughts or rather doubts about her, created pain. That must be nonsense. Yet he could not deny that he was glad that he was having David look into it.

Now, he saw Aubrey's car pulling in. She immediately jumped out of it, and skipped towards him, before giving him a gentle kiss on the cheek.

"How did your lesson go?" She asked.

"Good," Marcus replied. "What have you been up to?"

"I was just getting some food. I bought some snacks so we could have a trip out into the woods now, if that's okay?" I thought you would enjoy a trip out to see my family woods. I wanted you to understand that bear attacks are not a common thing around here."

"I think I understand that," said Marcus chuckling, "or at least I hope so anyway. But I would like to see these woods, especially if they are one's you grew up playing in."

"Great," said Aubrey. "We can go now, if you are good to do so? It's only half an hour from here, but it's in the opposite direction from that Fort, which Rusty showed us."

Aubrey was very happy on the journey down to her family woods, chattering away about the history of the area.

"My family, the Gibbet's, and the Tate's and the Mayhew's were the original settlers of this area. If you think this area is remote now, imagine what it was like then. To carve out any sort of living must have been rough. By all accounts, they arrived here around the 1740's, though we can't be sure of course. I am very proud of the fact that my family were pioneers." she said.

"That must have been an incredibly tough life. I am sure they were on the edge of starvation for much of it. At least until the crops they had started to regularly produce good yield," said Marcus.

"You have no idea what they had to do to survive", said Aubrey, her face suddenly darkening. "In today's society, things come so easily to people, food is everywhere. Technology and medicine are everywhere. Imagine if you were desperate though Marcus. And I don't mean just hungry. I mean imagine if you and your kids hadn't eaten properly for months, and those you love were weak from disease. Wouldn't you do what you needed to, just to survive?"

"I think I would do everything I could to keep me and my family alive," Marcus replied.

"Exactly!" said Aubrey, slamming her fist on the steering wheel with such passion that it caused him to jump. "You would do anything you needed to do! Anything! We reckon that about half the people who first came to settle here died. Maybe they made the wrong decisions, maybe they were unlucky, but they died! My people, and the Tate's, and the Mayhew's. We survived because we made the right one's! And even now, our families still run Ollenberry and the surrounding area."

"Almost like a clan thing?" said Marcus.

Aubrey smiled at this. "Yes, almost like that," she replied. Now, she turned down a dirt sidetrack and pulled up by some stone buildings.

"We are here," she said, "come and take a look."

Marcus counted seven roughly built stone buildings which seemed to be formed around a square, in which was a smaller building with an oval roof. All of them were in immaculate condition.

Aubrey anticipated the question "The families keep them maintained," she said. "We all contribute, both in labor and financially. We think it's imperative to maintain our heritage. To remember."

"I think it is wonderful, that you do." said Marcus.

"Thank you, babe." Aubrey shot him a smile as she spoke. Then she added, "come and walk down to the little creek with me, it's just a short way down the trail."

"Of course," Marcus replied. "I would love to."

The path leading down to the creek was beautiful. Purple and pink flowers adorned the path, their vibrant colors so bright, that they seemed to shimmer in the sunlight. The creek bubbled clear waters over verdant green rocks, while bright blue dragonflies swooped over its gentle banks.

"This is an amazingly beautiful place," said Marcus.

"Isn't it just!" Exclaimed Aubrey. "My ancestors fought for all of this. Now you can see that it was damn well worth fighting for."

Evil In Ollenberry

"I really can, "said Marcus.

"Hell, I might even let you drink some of that creek water one day," Aubrey joked. "It's the best damn water in the whole of the county. Not now, but one day, if you are very lucky." She winked as she said it, and then moved towards him very slowly, her hips swaying as she did so.

Silently, they took off each other's clothes, and merged into one...

"I have a surprise for you," said Aubrey, as she finished dressing.

"You are going to have to go some to beat what just happened," joked Marcus.

"A different kind of surprise," said Aubrey, arching her eyebrows as she did so. "I have my paranormal kit with me. There is an old graveyard nearby here. As it is going to get dark soon and it will be quiet, I thought we could do an investigation before we head home, if you like?"

"That sounds like a great idea," said Marcus. "Let's do it."

The graveyard was on top of a hill, through what to Marcus looked like ancient woodland. There were seemingly no houses for many miles around.

"How did a graveyard end up here, in such a remote spot?" said Marcus.

Evil In Ollenberry

"There was a plague here amongst my people, and many died at the same time", said Aubrey. "My ancestors decided to build one here away from any town to reduce the risk of contamination. We still own the land. Out of respect to them, we decided to forbid any further houses."

"That makes sense," said Marcus.

"They did what they had to do," said Aubrey, "as you now know. Anyway, let's get the equipment out. As well as the torches, I am going to use the EMF detector, and the REM pod. If things go well, I might try the Ganzfeld experiment out on you."

"What is that stuff all used for?" said Marcus.

"I could give you a long explanation, but I know you won't listen, so here is a shortened version," said Aubrey." The electromagnetic frequency will often spike when a spirit is around, and the detector will show that. It might give us clues as to where in the graveyard we should focus in on."

" We can use the REM pod to communicate with a spirit. I will ask questions, and the lights on the top will go off in response to them. The idea is that the spirit manipulates the lights to basically answer yes or no, to the questions I am asking.

With the 'Ganzfeld' experiment, I will place some headphones on you, which will be playing white noise. You can't hear the questions, but you should hopefully hear some words, randomly come through the noise at times. That could be the spirit talking to you. You just say, out loud, what you hear."

"I would certainly like to try that, it sounds like a lot of fun."

"It is," Aubrey replied, "and I promise you will really enjoy it. First though, let's use the detector to see if we can find any spots that may be of interest. Also, if you are drawn to a grave, then tell me, and we can focus in on that one."

"Okay," said Marcus, He observed the direction, in which Aubrey was walking.

"I will start looking"' he said. He then walked in the opposite direction of Aubrey's path.

"If you get any feelings, if you are drawn to a particular grave for whatever reason, then let me know and we will work on it," Aubrey shouted back to him as she walked away.

Marcus walked cautiously through the graves. He couldn't feel anything except the night chill. Aubrey had told him previously that most investigations like this end up with little happening, and in all probability, this would be one of those nights, so his expectations were low.

Evil In Ollenberry

The graveyard was in pristine condition. The grass was mowed, there were even fresh flowers placed in graves that were hundreds of years old, so they clearly couldn't be placed by relatives.

Now, he moved towards the farthest corner of the graveyard.As he moved closer, he experienced a tingling sensation in his fingers. The closer he moved to the corner, the stronger the feeling was. To test it, he tried moving away from the spot, and as he did so, his fingers began to stop tingling.

He followed the tingling feeling, noting where it was at its strongest, until he got to two particular graves.

Luke and Eleanor Johnson. They both appeared to have died within a few months of each other, in the 1860's. Now, he began feeling nauseous, and started retching. The feeling was so intense, that he spat bile out.

"What's going on, what's the matter?" said Aubrey.

"I felt a tingling in my fingers," said Marcus." I walked over here in response to it, and then I had this intense dizzy feeling almost straight away. I have never experienced anything like it before."

"That's fabulous!" Aubrey replied. "And the EMF reader is going off the charts. It seems like you have made a really strong connection here."

"Right now, it feels more like gastric flu than a strong connection," said Marcus jokingly.

Aubrey chuckled at this. Then she said, "I think we should try going straight into the Ganzfeld experiment. Remember, once I put the headphones on you won't be able to hear any questions I ask. Just speak out what you hear. If you hear nothing, then just sit there. When you have had enough, just let me know, and I will take them off for you. Have you got it?"

"Yes," said Marcus. "I understand."

"Right then," said Aubrey. "Here we go."

She placed the headphones on him. He could see that she was mouthing words to him, but he could hear nothing that she was saying, just loud static. Then Aubrey gave him the thumbs up sign, and he responded by giving it back to her. Now he concentrated, and the moment he did so, he heard a very clear `yes` through the headphones.

"Yes" Marcus said out loud. The voice sounded feminine. Maybe this was Eleanor? He speculated. Then, he began repeating what it said to him...

"It is me, Eleanor"

"The plague, it was the plague. The plague took both of our lives. "

"I wish you could communicate with Lucas. He refuses to come forward to speak to you now, because he is very stubborn.

"Immediately after my earthly body was finally overwhelmed by the plague, I 'passed over'. I experienced no pain, and honestly I felt wonderful, as soon as I passed."

There was no sick body, dragging me down. I experienced a true freedom to be rid of the restraints of my fleshly body.

"I" still existed. "Me", Eleanor, is still here and unchanged. If that makes sense..." said Eleanor.

"A physical body," is not necessary to still exist, I soon found out. I had passed into 'another world', for lack of better description. It was a different dimension," she said

"Oh, how badly I wanted to go into the beautiful, comforting 'Light', after I left my earthly body." said Eleanor

"I just would not let the 'light' draw me away from my Lucas. I knew death would come soon, and take him. I knew he would be with me, after his death, so I waited, I did not follow the 'Light." I resisted.

"I course," said Eleanor, " assumed that Lucas would go 'Into the 'Light,' and I would go with him, towards the feeling of peace."

" Lucas refused to go, and I felt that I could not leave him." she said. " So, there you go, that is why we are 'stuck' here, in what feels like 'limbo.' That is our story."

Marcus suddenly stopped. He felt that same pain in his head and fuzziness that he had had when talking to his friend David. Then, a different voice came through.

"Marcus, it's me Katy! Whatever you do, don't repeat what I am saying. Do you understand? " said Katy.

"Yes," said Marcus out loud.

"I said don't repeat what I am saying!" said Katy. "You don't remember me right now, but you know something is wrong. In a minute, you are going to take off the headphones and walk towards the other side of the graveyard. Aubrey has used witchcraft to make you forget me."

"I will make you remember. When you do, you must act normally. DO NOT let Aubrey know that you remember. If she does, you are finished. Just nod if you understand." said, the

Marcus had no idea what was going on, but his instinct told him to trust the voice, so he gave the slightest of nods. He could see Aubrey looking puzzled.

"Alright then," said Katy. "Anymore talking between us and she will catch on. I know you have your doubts, but just go with it. You haven't got anything to lose."

Marcus took his headphones off and blinked hard.

"How did I do?" He said.

" You were great," Aubrey replied. "You certainly made a connection with Eleanor. The responses you got from her were impressive."

"Did she say anything interesting?" Marcus replied. "It was difficult to understand what was happening as I was only repeating the answers to your questions."

"Yes," Aubrey replied. "It seems that she and he husband, both died of the plague, which was not a surprise, given the times she was living in. That was the worst time of all, for our families, even harder than when we first settled here. Can you imagine how it felt?"

"I can't even begin to," said Marcus. "I am sorry that they had to suffer so much."

"Yes, they did," said Aubrey. "It was horrendous. And, the things they needed to do to survive... They did those things, because it was necessary, they had no regrets."

Now she looked at him carefully, as if reading him, she said, "Are you okay though, babe. Did the experiment freak you out a bit? You started to make no sense towards the end of it. Are you ready to go home now?"

"I just got a bit confused towards the end, that's all," said Marcus, "but I am feeling okay. I think I just might walk it off a bit for a minute if that's alright with you?"

"Of course," Aubrey replied. "I will just pack up, while you are doing that, and then we can be on our way."

Aubrey began walking towards the car with the equipment, and as she did so, Marcus turned and walked in the opposite direction as quickly as he could.

As soon as he reached the graveyard boundary, he whispered into the tree line, "I am here." He felt ridiculous, but so much strange stuff had happened, since he had moved to Ollenberry.

"And, so am I!" said an old woman, who he instantly recognized as Katy, slid quickly from behind a tree.

"Katy!" said Marcus. "You are the old woman I saw when I was in town. You said if I ever needed you, to say, "Katy come and get me," three times and you would appear."

"Yes, that's right. Said Katy, "and I wish you had trusted me enough to say it when you tried to escape, but I understand that supernatural things are new to you. I don't have much time, though, if Aubrey sees me talking to you, then you are dead." With that, she waved her hand, and a gold mist swept over his body. At that moment, he remembered.

He remembered the fire pit, and the names in the dust. He remembered what Ed had told him about the disappearance of that man Simon Cornish, and he remembered about the bizarre Bigfoot attack. He remembered it all, in one sharp painful flash.

He staggered back, trying to suck in air that would not fill his lungs, and as he did so, Katy grabbed him.

"Breathe," Katy said soothingly. "I know it hurts. I am sorry that I couldn't be more gentle. If I didn't restore your memories this way, then you would have taken ages to remember them."

"Are you ready to listen now Marcus?" said Katy." I can see that she is almost finished packing up that car, and she will come looking for you in a minute."

"I am ready to listen," said Marcus.

"Good!" exclaimed Katy. "Now the next time you see me, I will appear like this".

Suddenly the face of the old woman melted away, and a young beautiful woman with long red hair appeared in front of him.

Katy smiled at him. "We are all young, and some of us are lucky enough to get old. Our appearance changes as we age, that is just the way of things. Some of my kind can appear as we wish to. I thought you might connect with the old woman, as being wise, when I first met you in the town center. That is why I appeared as I did."

"I think though you would be better served by me appearing as I choose to appear, which is like this."

"I will certainly remember you," said Marcus, "you are lovely, if you don't mind me saying."

"Not at all," Katy replied. "Now, listen quickly. A challenge for you is coming soon at that fancy dress party. It will be extremely difficult, and there is a very high probability that you will fail. If you don't succeed, then you will not make it out of this town alive."

"Oh great," said Marcus. "I might as well just dig my spot here and lie down in then".

"Ha Ha!" Katy said, "Not quite, because I can help you. Just summon me when you find yourself in trouble. Yes, you will definitely have some trouble, for sure."

"And, do you know exactly what kind of trouble, I will find myself in?" said Marcus.

"No, I don't," she said. "I can tell you that it will have something to do with the fancy dress costume that you chose. All of the others chose to go into the clothes shop in town, as well."

"All the others, what do you mean?" said Marcus anxiously.

"There were others before you that they brought here. You already have guessed what happened to them," said Katie.

"I want you to be the last." then she added, "Now, you need to act normal at Tate's when you start working there. Be a good employee, don't give them any reason to suspect you have your memory back."

Katy disappeared instantly, just as Aubrey started striding towards him. That was no coincidence, Marcus thought.

"Are you feeling better Babe, are you ready to go?" said Aubrey.

"Yes, I am good," said Marcus. "Let's go."

"Excellent," said Aubrey. "Let's go home then. I would say it has been a pretty amazing day."

Evil In Ollenberry

"And I would agree," said Marcus.

The next day, Marcus got up late. He would be sorry to say goodbye to his students. He regretted ever leaving Los Angeles. But it was done now, and he had to get himself out of this perilous mess that he had found himself in. He checked his lesson plan, and then switched on his Zoom.

His students were already waiting for him, which was unusual. "Good morning you guys," said Marcus, as he checked them in. "It is good to have you here for what will be out last lesson together. Today we are going to have a test and recap on our business language, and we will also play a game."

Adam, Cindy and Max all said good morning in unison. It was Max that spoke first.

"Teacher," said Max, "as it is our last lesson, we wanted to show you something that happened yesterday, something that surprised us."

"Yes," added Adam, "it really shocked us. We all heard it, but we couldn't be sure. It was only when Cindy played it back that we could be sure."

"What is it?" asked Marcus. "As Adam said," Cindy began nervously. "We all heard it, so I decided to record it. Can, I play it for you, is that okay?"

"Yes, absolutely," said Marcus, a little bemused, "please play what you heard."

As he spoke, he gave Cindy control of the meeting. "First of all, we all heard this. Not just at the beginning of the lesson, but throughout it."

It was unmistakable. The screeching of tortured souls. They screamed their despair. It sounded like they were in pain. Desperate, they seemed to bellow from the darkness. It was a frightening and hollow sound, that made Marcus shudder involuntarily.

"Do you remember hearing this? "said Cindy. "I have cleaned it up a bit, but as you can hear, it was definitely there. We wondered if it might be a trick you were playing or something."

"No," said Marcus. "I heard nothing at all. If I had heard that, I guarantee that I would have stopped the lesson. That's horrific."

"We thought so," said Cindy, "but we wanted to check. Then she added, "but it gets creepier."

"Creepier!" Marcus said in response. "How could it get creepier!"

"You will see," said Cindy.

Evil In Ollenberry

Cindy then played back a clip from yesterday's lesson. Marcus was talking about the business. Then suddenly, the doll behind him its head around! The porcelain doll! Sharp to the right! There was no mistaking it!

"What do you think of this?" said Cindy.

"I have no idea," said Marcus. He was shocked. Immediately, he swung around to look at the doll. It stood there, impassive.

"It is the most incredible thing I have ever seen," said Cindy. "I want to put it on Instagram."

Marcus stopped himself from commenting on the fact that their reaction had been to put it on Instagram. That was normal with today's young people. They had waited, they had asked him first and now he needed their help.

"It certainly is remarkable, what can I say? Please can I ask you not to put it on Instagram for now though? I need to investigate it. Can you give me a couple of weeks to look into it? If I find out something before then, I will let you know. If I don't, then you can put it up anyway? Do we have a deal?" asked Marcus.

"We have a deal, teacher." said Cindy. "Only because you are my favorite teacher though."

"Thank you all," said Marcus.

"You need to get out of there though teacher, it's a bad place," said Cindy.

"Yes, I agree with Cindy," said Adam, "please get out of there."

"We were so worried about you," added Max. "We will hear from you then, by no later than two weeks from today?"

"I promise you will," Marcus said.

When the lesson was over, Marcus packed away his teaching materials for the last time, giving the doll careful scrutiny as he did so, but it remained static. He was glad when he got out of the room.

In a way, what the students had heard was a good thing. If anything did happen to him, the students would be plastering it all over social media, and the town of Ollenberry would at the very least, get the kind of scrutiny that it so desperately wanted to avoid. It did give him a time limit though. Two weeks. It didn't seem enough, but then he was always at his best when he worked against deadlines.

***

Ed blinked hard. He was fighting sleep now. Normally he wouldn't push himself like this, he would have stopped hours ago. He was beyond keen to make it to Marcus though. His friend was in terrible danger, and Ed knew he had to pull Marcus out of that terrible situation.

Nonetheless, he would have to stop now. He needed rest. If he slept now, and then pushed it, he would reach Marcus by tomorrow. He scanned for motels, and there was a sign for one, just ten miles ahead. It was better than sleeping in his car, he reckoned. He pulled off of the freeway, and headed down a backcountry lane, to the local motel in a little town

At first, he didn't believe that he had seen it. He was tired, and it had, after all, disturbed him badly the first time he had seen it. He carried on, now pushing the car much harder than he had before though, just in case. It was only a few more miles into town.

At first, he had thought it was his tires. A large boom caused his car to swerve. Ed fought desperately now, to keep his car on the road.

The car spluttered, and as it did so, huge plumes of smoke billowed out of his hood.

"Dammit," Ed shouted out loud. He pulled up and got out of the car.

The car hood was completely smashed in. The engine was wrecked. It looked like a gigantic boulder had been dropped on it. The car wasn't going anywhere that night, thought Ed. Indeed, it looked like it would never work again. He would have to walk into town, and deal with it tomorrow, he thought. There was no way a tow truck would come out tonight.

He just managed to get a glimpse of it, before the bolt hit him. He just had time to swerve his body to one side.

He was lying on the ground now. The pain was so sickening, that his body jolted with it. His eyelids were heavy. He wanted to keep them open, but it was just too much. Just before he closed them though, he saw it. That damn cloud. It hovered over him for just a few seconds. Checking. Then it shot off into the night...

***

"Have a great day at work, my love," said Aubrey, as she dropped him off at Tates.

"I will try my best," said Marcus.

"You will be your best," said Aubrey, as she drove off.

Marcus tried to focus now and play a part. Either way, he wouldn't be at Tate's all that long. He was going to escape or be dead. There was no in between for him, and he knew that. He normally tried to do a good job in the places he worked, he was no slacker. Here though he had no motivation to work hard. Except that he had to play a part, and not arouse suspicion.

He walked up to the desk. The pink haired girl was there, but this time she wasn't looking bored. Indeed, she watched him very carefully as he approached.

How can I help you today?" she said.

"I am here to see Mr. Tate. I am the new starter." he said.

"Oh, you are getting a personal tour off Mr. Tate himself, as a new starter. You must be important," she said jokingly.

There was another woman, standing next to her behind the desk. She whispered to her way too loudly, so that Marcus could overhear, "he is connected to one of the three founding families. Go and get Mr. Tate."

The pink haired girl turned pale. Then she stammered, "yes, I will get him. I am sorry Dee," she said turning to the woman beside her. "I am sorry, Marcus."

"No problem at all," said Marcus.

Mr. Tate came striding towards him, his huge frame making them all look like dwarves.

"Good to see you, Marcus," said Mr. Tate. "Welcome to the store."

Evil In Ollenberry

"Thank you, sir," said Marcus. "I am keen to learn."

"And we are keen for you to do so", Mr. Tate replied. "Here at Tate's the motto is all about family. Family first. And you are a very important part of that. Now let me give you a brief introduction to the business, before leaving you with your new team members."

"Thank you, sir," said Marcus.

"And at Tate's, we leave no stone unturned when it comes to customer service. Any little attention to detail, becomes the bigger detail, becomes the bigger picture. It can become the whole world, can't it?" said Mr. Tate.

"I guess," said Marcus, having no idea what he was talking about.

"Let me give you an example, said Mr. Tate. "We sell screws here at Tate's, of course we do. The difference is though that we are passionate about what we do. All companies say that about what they do, I know that, but we MEAN it."

"So, our team members don't just sell a screw. They are PART of the screw. They are with it, when it is selected from the packet. They are with it when it screws in ever so tightly, making a hole deep into the unwilling wood. Making it good. Making it good wood. That's what our team members do." said Mr. Tate.

"We CARE here. That's what amazing customer service is all about." said Mr. Tate.

He paused to look at Marcus now, whose face remained impassive, despite his desire to break out into a laugh. Instead, he managed a nod at Mr. Tate.

"We also sell washing machines here," Billy runs that department, said Mr. Tate. "He is great at sales. If you ask him what his secret is, he will tell you, that he climbs inside the washing machines with the customer and holds hands with them, in a virtual sense of course. Then, they all tumble around, spinning together with the dirty laundry, before being reborn new and clean. He paints a picture for the customer, and they love it. They fall into his arms."

"I have no doubt, that they will fall into your arms. When they do Marcus, catch them, catch them like newborn baby cubs. Then, you will have a customer who is a tiger for you. They will be roaring their praises of you, for an eternity," said Mr. Tate.

"I can't wait," said Marcus, trying to make the sarcasm in his voice as imperceptible as he could.

"Good", said Mr. Tate. "Very good. Now, I did think about starting you in lumber, but Cameron does his own weird thing with the wood. I don't think you are ready for all that yet. It's a bit complicated for a beginner."

"So, I am putting you with Tara in windows and doors. She really knows her stuff, and she will help you. Your manager is Gen. You won't meet her until next week, after the fancy dress party. She is thorough though. She will help you." said Mr. Tate.

"Now, I will leave you with Tara." said Mr. Tate.

With that, Mr. Tate strode over to the back of the store, with Marcus following behind him. Behind a desk, and unsurprisingly flanked on either side, stood a petite and very attractive woman with shoulder length brown hair.

As she saw them approach, Tara immediately shot out from behind her desk. They exchanged greetings, and then Mr. Tate said,

"I will leave you to it, enjoy your time at Tate's. Be good to the wood."

"I will," said Marcus. "The wood and I are one. We grow together."

"Excellent," said Mr. Tate. "You are learning fast."

Now Tara turned to Marcus and said, "you are connected to the three founding families I hear. Your fiancé, is Aubrey, is it not?"

"Yes, that's right," said Marcus.

"That is quite a pedigree, she replied. "Good for you. You know, we are all connected with them in some way here at Tate's. To a greater or lesser extent. There is no time to waste though. Now let me tell you about doors and windows."

Marcus listened politely as Tara explained to him the various minutae associated with the products. Really though, he was interested in anything that might give him an opportunity to get out of Ollenberry.

He wanted to get out of Ollenberry, as fast as possible. He was interested in any quirks of their society that he could absorb, so he could best understand them.

After lunch, Tara tasked him with loading doors up for customers in the parking lot. While he was while he was doing that, he noticed a short man scurrying across the lot. The man was dressed entirely in a black suit, with a straw hat. Behind him trailed a woman. She was also dressed in black, with a tight black bonnet stretched around her head, and a long black shawl draped around her shoulders.

It wasn't just the way the man was dressed that interested him. It was his movements. He appeared almost furtive, as though he was hiding from something.

"He belongs to the Clamash," said Tara. "They are outsiders here. They shun modern technology. They always have. Apparently, they arrived around the same time as the first families."

"They took a different path though, as you can see. They don't really like us. But, they have to deal, in some ways, with modern technology. They come into Tate's, and leave as quickly as they can." said Tara.

Then, the Clamash man turned to look at Marcus, stopping suddenly, as he did so. He looked like an animal caught in car headlights. Then, he whispered something to the woman who had bumped into him. Now, they both turned to stare directly at him.

"What are they doing?" Marcus asked.

"They are staring at you," said Tara.

"I have no idea why," Tara replied. "If you are asking me to come up with an explanation, then I don't have an answer. It's very unusual."

Marcus was satisfied with his first day at Tate's. Tomorrow, Tara had promised to take him on a more detailed tour of the place. That might give him an opportunity to look for more information about the families.

He also resolved to seek an opportunity to speak to the Clamash, if he possibly could. If they were alienated from the society here, then they might become allies. And, he needed allies badly.

"How did your first day at work go?" said Aubrey, after she picked him up.

"Great," Marcus replied. "Mr. Tate gave me a talk on customer service, and then he introduced to my work colleagues. I am going to be mostly working with a young lady called Tara, selling windows and doors."

"That's great," said Aubrey. "I am really glad it went well."

"I had a question for you," said Marcus. "There was a couple I saw in the parking lot, wearing old fashioned black clothing. Tara said they were from something called the Clamash."

"She said they were best avoided, and then we got back to work as we were busy. I wondered what your opinion was on them." said Marcus.

"Tara is right," snapped Aubrey. "They rejected the views of the three families, and as a result, find themselves at the bottom of society here. They are very unlikely to even speak to you. They consider us to be polluted."

"Polluted? What does that mean?" said Marcus.

"According to them, we are polluted by our desires. Our needs have overtaken us. Warped our relationship with the natural world, or something like that. For example, they avoid our technology as much as they can. In any event, they won't speak to you unless they have to." said Aubrey.

"Anyway, I wanted to show you my costume for the fancy dress. I hope you will like it." Aubrey said.

They went inside the house, and Aubrey went to change. A few minutes later, she emerged in a long silk dress, resplendent with a purple corset.

"I thought you would enjoy this," she said. "I wanted to keep the cowboy theme up that you chose. The kids have got costumes from the same period too. What do you think?"

"I think you look fabulous, and I am very lucky indeed," said Marcus.

"There is a prize for the best family in the competition, and I think we could win it. I hope we will." Aubrey replied.

The buzz at Tate's the next day was all about the fancy dress party. It was weird to Marcus that the whole place was so obsessed by it, but then there was nothing normal to this town, Marcus thought.

He began doing safety checks down the aisles, as Tara was on a later shift. Then he saw him. At the bottom of the aisle, stood a Clamash man from yesterday, just staring at him.

The man scurried away and began conversing with another much older man with a white beard. This man had two women standing by his side, one of whom he recognized from the previous day. All of them were dressed in the same dour black costume of the Clamash.

Marcus looked straight back at them. To his surprise, they now moved forward towards him, and surrounded him in a circle.

"Can I help you?" said Marcus.

"Could he do it?" said the young woman, "what do you think, elder?"

Marcus noticed that the oldest man was squinting at him hard. As if trying to see beyond his physical appearance, and this made him feel very uncomfortable. "He could. There is a chance."

In response to this, the other Clamash burst into radiant smiles.

Evil In Ollenberry

The elder held up his hand to silence them. Then he said, "only a chance, mind you. There has not been one in a long time like him though. So, we will give it to him. "

"Excuse me," said Marcus. "What are you talking about?"

Now, the elder took something from his pocket, a small object, wrapped in a white cloth. He unwrapped it carefully. It was a small turquoise stone, which he placed carefully in the palm of his hand.

"Please take it," said the elder. "Squeeze it when you are in need, and we will come. You will understand when."

"I will take it with much thanks," said Marcus.

The Elder, looked at him and nodded. Then the Clamash all melted away as quickly as they had come.

"What was all that about," said Billy, "I was just coming over to see if you were okay with the safety checks, and I saw them surrounding you."

"They were just getting some advice off me about a new window product that's just come in," said Marcus.

"Uh huh," Billy replied, "well that is a niche market you can pick up. They won't have anything to do with the rest of us."

The fancy dress party was to be held in the town hall, a large red brick building in the center of town. As they approached it, Marcus could see that it was adorned with torches.

"The original town hall building burnt down," said Aubrey. "For us, this is a very modern addition to our town."

"Is adorning it with torches, a good thing?" said Marcus. "You don't want to tempt fate."

Aubrey laughed at this, and then she said, "fate can be twisted. You will see. Will is always much stronger than fate, if you are determined enough. That is what we all believe."

The entrance was guarded by four men who were dressed as roman soldiers. They scrutinized each individual ticket very thoroughly before allowing any individual in.

"Security is tight here, for a fancy dress party," Marcus remarked.

"Indeed, it is," said Aubrey. "Only the families are allowed inside."

They walked through the entrance, and into a huge dining room. It was ornately and gaudily decorated, with gold paneling and rich purple and red tapestries on the walls. The room was dimly lit, just like Mr. Tate's office, Marcus thought. Rows of circular tables were covered in bleached white lacy tablecloths.

"Let's find our table," said Aubrey, "it will be near the top of the room, towards Mr. Tate's table."

At the far end of the room was a rectangular table, which was raised off the ground by a platform. Stairs led up to it, in either direction. Marcus guessed that that must be where Mr. Tate would be, when he walked in.

They were not late, but the place was already full. There was an excited chatter in the air. As he passed the tables, he saw people turn towards him. There were quite a few Vikings he noted, as well as the obligatory pirates and clowns.

Aubrey had dashed ahead of him, and began waving to him that she had found their table. To his surprise, there were already two people at it.

A man and a woman stood together. They were also dressed in the same period costume as him, and both of them stood up to greet him as they approached. The man was dressed as a cowboy, with a pinstriped jacket, black Stetson and boots with silver spurs. The woman was dressed in the same fashion as Aubrey, the only difference being that she wore a red corset. She also sported a red ostrich feather in her hair as opposed to Aubrey's purple one. Other than that, their outfits were identical.

"I would like you to meet Mr. Abraham Knox and his wife Sarah," said Aubrey.

The man was tall and wiry, with hard thin face. Unlike anyone else he had seen in the town, Mr. Knox sported a long white handlebar moustache. His wife had long blonde hair. She had only just managed to squeeze into her corset, from the looks of things, as her breasts were almost spilling over the top of them.

"How do you do," said Mr. Knox. "I am Abe, and as you heard, this is my wife, Sarah. We have known Aubrey for a very long time, so we are very happy to be at a table with you all today."

"Now the pleasantries are over, let's pour some wine!" exclaimed Sarah, giggling as she did so.

They all sat down, while Sarah poured the wine. Aubrey turned to chat to Sarah leaving Marcus to chat to Abe.

"So, how do you like our small town?" said Abe.

"I like it very much indeed," said Marcus. "Everyone seems to be related to one another, which is unusual to say the least, that they have all stayed in one place. It's very friendly though, people have been kind to me."

"It's a unique strength that keeps us all together," said Abe. "The suffering our families endured brought us together and made us strong. It bonded us."

"I can understand that," said Marcus, "but that was hundreds of years ago. Things have changed."

"We have always considered diversity a pollutant, it warps us." said Abe. "Men are weak now, their masculinity subsumed. Women cannot be women, they have to act like men or be crushed. We don't think that is right, not right at all," said Abe, shaking his head as he did so.

"I accept though, that some change has to come. The families cannot carry on everything exactly as it was, not all the way through time. They become stretched thin, you see? Like if you watered down this wine. Sometimes, we need new blood, just like you need new vineyards to grow the grapes on. The trick is to be very careful with the grapes you select though. Very careful indeed. You don't want them polluting the crop. So, you have to be thorough, test plenty. Only when you have got just the right one, can you add it to the others to be pressed. Do you see what I mean, Marcus?"

Marcus's imperative was to gather information, not engage in this kind of very uncomfortable discussion, as much as he wanted to. So, he sidestepped the question.

"So, what do you do here in town, Abe?" Marcus said.

"My family was the original enforcer for the families," Abe replied. "We guarded the town as it was being built. We organized the lawmen, helped to deal with all types of unsavory characters all the way through history. We were good at it, as you can see. We have all prospered under Mr. Tate." said Abraham.

"You mean Mr. Tate's ancestor's," said Marcus.

"Exactly," said Abe smiling. "Under his ancestors everyone did well." Then he added, "and, I still keep that role even today. I am watchful of things. I correct any kinks, when that needs to be done."

At that point, the centurions entered, together with some small boys. The boys were carrying silver trays, on which were placed small shot glasses, which contained a clear liquid. The boys began passing them out as they moved around the tables.

"Don't drink it until Mr. Tate says so," said Aubrey. "It's for the toast."

Once the drinks had been given out, Mr. Tate entered the room. Then, everyone stood up in silence as he did so.

He was completely alone on his table at the top, Marcus noted, except for two chairs on either side of him, which were empty.

Then Mr. Tate raised his glass. He looked across the attentive crowd.

"Tonight, is truly a special night," he said. "Not just for our community as an important social occasion, but because we have the potential for a new family member to join us. Very rarely do any of them come this far, once a decade maybe. And, none have ever passed this test. Yet they must, for it is our way. To join us is a bountiful reward, which outsiders cannot possibly comprehend. And so, they must pass this test."

With that, he raised his glass, and said, "ladies and gentlemen, I give you the test!"

"To the test!" The crowd shouted, and with that, everyone drank their shot.

Marcus did the same. The drink tasted foul, like tepid foul water. Yet it burned his throat when it went down.

"What the hell is this?" he said to Aubrey. His legs collapsed on him now, and he clung onto the table for support. He tried to speak, but he found that no matter how hard he tried, words would not come out. He noticed that the entire room was looking at him now, but nobody seemed to be moving to help him, not even Aubrey.

He had no strength left, and he fell to the ground. The last thing he heard was another thud beside him. Somebody else had fallen too...

Marcus moved his head slowly and opened his eyes. His body hurt, And his eyes stung against the bright intensity of the sun. The sun, he thought? He was inside a dining hall, how could he see the sun. He got to his knees and looked around.

He wasn't in the dining hall anymore. He was standing in a dusty square. Surrounding it were wooden shops. He could see that there was a grocery store, a barber's shop, and a saloon. Straight in front of him was a crooked wooden clock tower. Its hands were showing that it was just a few minutes to noon. He spun around, confused, trying to absorb where he was.

"Hello," he said. "Is anyone there?"

Silence.

"Aubrey? Aubrey are you here?" He listened again, but there was no response.

He looked down at his waist. Around it was a gun belt, and a pistol. Slowly, he drew the pistol and saw that it was loaded.

Evil In Ollenberry

He had no difficulty now in processing what awaited him. He was here for some kind of showdown. A street fight, no doubt. And given that he had fired a handgun on only a couple of occasions before, and that was years ago, he stood very little chance. "Screw this," he said out loud.

He ran for cover towards the barber's shop with the gun still drawn. It was opposite the saloon, where he reckoned his assailant must be, if his knowledge of old-fashioned westerns was anything to go by.

Sure enough, from the gloomy darkness of the saloon, a figure emerged. Marcus instantly realized who it was. It was Abe.

"Now don't be like that," said Abe. "If you start hiding and all, this may take longer than it needs to, and I am a very hungry man. You have a pistol, I have a pistol. The odds are even."

"The odds are not even. You bastard!" shouted Marcus. "I have hardly held one of these damn things in my entire life!"

Abe turned to him and smiled. "All you need to do, is squeeze the trigger, aim and fire, like this."

Boom! A shot rang out, and Marcus felt a searing heat pierce into his stomach. He immediately fired a shot off in Abe's direction, who ducked in response. Marcus staggered into the barber's shop. It was deserted. He spun around as he gripped the chair, knocking over a shotgun that was placed on the countertop next to some razors.

Abe had begun to advance, so Marcus fired another shot, this time much closer to Abe, which caused him to retreat back to the saloon.

"That was much closer," shouted Abe. "I think you are fatally wounded though, so I will just wait."

Marcus fell to his knees. "Katy come and get me, Katy come and get me, Katy come and get me!" He shouted.

Instantly Katy appeared. Then she said, "Grab the honey from your pocket, quick now, and pour it on the wound. It will heal you."

Marcus did as she had instructed. "This honey will heal my wound?" He asked.

"None of this is as it seems Marcus, so yes, it will." She quickly replied. "Now get ready to turn the dial on your watch. That will reset the scene. And give you another chance at beating him."

"I don't want another chance at beating him, I just want you to get me the hell out of here." said Marcus.

Evil In Ollenberry

"I can't do that. You are stuck here, the only way out is to beat him or die. And if you die here, you will die in the real world too."

Marcus heard steps. Abe was approaching.

"And, how to I do that? He is some kind of professional gunfighter?" said Marcus.

"This test isn't designed so that it is impossible for you to win," said Katy. "It's designed, so that it is very, very difficult for you to do so. He has to have a weakness, or there has to be an edge you have. Think of what the opportunities are, and use them."

"Where are you," Marcus? said Abe. "I am a generous man, and I have decided to put you out of your misery."

Marcus twisted the dial on his watch.

He pulled himself to his feet, and spun around. This time, he didn't call out. He reckoned he only had a few seconds left, before Abe came out anyway, so he ran straight to the barber's shop and grabbed the shotgun. He positioned himself behind a water barrel and waited.

"Where are you, Marcus? said Abe. "Let's not waste time. I am a professional and you are an amateur."

Good, thought Marcus. He has no recollection of what happened before. Marcus

Evil In Ollenberry

aimed the shotgun and fired. He was close, with the saloon doors by Abe's, head splintering as they accommodated the huge hole that now shone through them."

"Whoa, that was close," said Abe, "But, not close enough, and now I know where you are."

This time, the shot hit him in the neck. Marcus clutched at it, as he fought not to pass out. His blood felt sticky as it mixed with the honey.

As he fumbled to turn the dial on his watch, he realized that he had almost run out. He couldn't afford another loss.

He got to his feet and ran straight to the barber's shop. He turned now, and sprinted straight to the grocery store, which was opposite the saloon.

"You are a smart man. I am sure you have already figured this out," said Abe, as he came out of the saloon. "Let's just get this over with."

Marcus aimed the shotgun and fired. This time, it made contact. Just nicking Abe's arm, but enough to make him bleed. Abe seemed startled by this, but quickly regained his composure. Abe was squinting, as he searched for where Marcus was hiding at the front of the grocery store.

These families, or whatever they are, hate bright light, Marcus thought. I was right. Abe can't see me.

Now, he brought his gun up carefully and slowly aiming straight at Abe's chest as he did so. The shot exploded into a ball of fire and blood, sending Abe flying backwards. As he did so, his gun spun away from him.

Marcus threw the shotgun to the ground and began running towards Abe, who now lay motionless on the ground.

Abe raised his head a little, as Marcus approached.

"Now can't you just let me be?" said Abe. "I can hardly move now, can I?"

"That is exactly what any reasonable person would do, and certainly what I would do," said Marcus. "Show compassion for the wounded. Yet, I think that your people would see that as a weakness, and you would try to kill me again. Why should I allow you to live?"

Abe chuckled at this, and began very slowly pulling out a small silver one shot pistol from a pocket on his waistcoat.

Before he could aim it though, Marcus shot him straight in the face.

Now, the world that he was in began to fade, as though someone was stripping it. First colors disappeared, and then he watched as the buildings started to crumble. The barbers shop folded into itself like cardboard, and the clock tower toppled into nothingness.

As soon as it did so, he could see the party beyond it. The dining room was clearly lit, opposed the monochrome world that he was now in. He could see Aubrey now waving to him.

"Come forward now, my love! Quick though! Do it now!"

He didn't hesitate, jumping straight through the light, and straight into the arms of Aubrey. He collapsed into them, stifling a sob as he did so.

Abe materialized on the floor next to him, and instantly began coughing. His wife Sarah rushed to his side, and holding his head in one of her hands, began to give him sips of water.

Then, the whole crowd gave a roar! The centurions blasted their trumpets, and men and women began dancing with each other on top of the tables.

Against this backdrop, Mr. Tate shouted, "let this party really begin!" The moment he announced this, women dressed as ancient Greeks, appeared carrying large jugs of red wine. The excited crowd guzzled the wine greedily.

"What just happened to me, Aubrey?" said Marcus. Then he added, "Hell, what is happening now?"

"You beat Abe!" said Aubrey. "That has not happened in generations! Nobody beats Abe! He is the greatest of fighters! Oh, my love, you have succeeded! Wonderful, with you being a modern-day city boy! I thought I would lose you tonight! We all did, and it would have been such a tragedy! You made it though, you passed the test!"

Abe had got to his feet now, and he limped over to where Marcus was, helped by Sarah. "You did the right thing shooting me in the face. I would have turned that dainty little pistol straight on you, had you given me just a few seconds longer."

"I figured that sort of ruthlessness was what was needed, to get the job done. To win," said Marcus.

"And, you figured absolutely right," said Abe. "We need that will to survive, to survive at all costs. That's what makes the families strong."

He patted Marcus on the back. Marcus didn't respond, instead he turned to Aubrey and said "I do need to know what happened, Aubrey. You owe me that much."

"Today's society never lives in the present," she sighed. "Modern folk are always concerning themselves. Worrying about what cannot be changed, or imagining future scenarios, that have little possibility of happening. Years wasted on hypothetical nonsense. Yet you will learn to live in the now, my love. I am sure of it."

"The present tastes so much sweeter if you savor it, rather than just pass through it, don't you see? In answer to your question, that was a test. A test which you passed. You already know that though."

"I will go through what happens next, tomorrow, is that okay?" she said, and then gave him a lingering kiss.

"That will do for now, I guess," said Marcus. He knew Aubrey was stubborn, and that would be her final word on the matter. Plus, right now, what he needed was a drink.

A smiling Aubrey took hold of his hand, and led him through the tables. He was cheered and clapped, as he passed by the tables.

At the back of the hall, on a nod from Aubrey, two centurions opened the doors to reveal a dance floor.

Then, Aubrey grabbed two glasses of wine, from one of the Greek serving girls, and handed one to Marcus.

"Here, drink this," she said.

"Really?" said Marcus, frowning at her.

"Really," said Aubrey laughing. "In one, with me."

Marcus guzzled the wine down. Now, he felt deliriously happy, and he joined Aubrey on the dancefloor. She was an excellent dancer, and she moved like liquid, as she swept across the dance floor.

Marcus danced too, and soon a circle had formed around them. He was enjoying one of the best moments of his life. It was Aubrey, who had to eventually drag him off the dance floor.

"You see how much sweeter that moment was," said Aubrey?

"Was it about the wine," said Marcus? "I feel amazing even now! Considering what I went through, I should be collapsing. But, I could go all night."

"The wine has a sort of magic in it," Aubrey admitted. "It amplifies feelings though, it doesn't create them. You are living in the present, enjoying your moment and enjoying my love."

She then paused to stare up at him, and said, "And, we shall dance and party until we are done!"

Marcus took her hand. She twirled again, laughing as she did so.

And then, they danced.

They danced until the morning, as did everyone else at the party. No one left, until Marcus and Aubrey had left the dance floor.

CHAPTER NINE

-The Initiation-

Ed moved his tongue around his mouth, very slowly. He could feel it. Next, he wiggled his toes, and then he moved his arms. Finally and reluctantly, he opened his eyes. And, it was hard work to do so.

He was in a hospital room, attached to a bleeping monitor of some kind. He was alive. The cloud had not killed him. That swerve to the side, just before the bolt hit him, had probably taken some of the sting out of the lightning bolt. Otherwise he would now be enjoying the afterlife, he considered.

"It's good to see you are awake," said the nurse. She was walking towards him. "You have been out quite a while," she said.

"How long?" Ed rasped.

"Well, we are not quite sure how long you have been unconscious," said the nurse. "An old couple found you prostrate in the road. All factors indicate, that you have been unconscious for approximately twenty-four hours. "

"The physicians have determined, that you were struck by lightning. They came to this diagnosis, after examining what your body seems to have gone through."

"Am I okay?" said Ed. "Yes," said the nurse, "you are perfectly fine, you just need a day of rest. You are quite the miracle though. We can't believe you have recovered so quickly."

"I don't have time for rest," said Ed. "I have to help my friend. He's in terrible danger."

"You could try calling him, and check he is okay, if you like? The old couple found your phone by your side, and handed it the paramedics when they arrived. It's amazing, that the phone wasn't fried. You must have dropped it, just before the bolt hit. You are lucky."

"I wouldn't exactly describe my situation as lucky, but I take your point," said Ed.

The nurse laughed at this, and then said. "I will go and get the Doctor, while you make your call. I shouldn't be more than five minutes."

Ed dialed Marcus's number and got straight through. First, he told him about the attack by the cloud. Then, he listened as Marcus explained the events of the previous night.

"That is insane!" Ed exclaimed. "We are both incredibly lucky to be alive."

"I know it's not a competition," said Marcus, "but I do think you got the worst of it.

Evil In Ollenberry

After I survived my test, I have to admit I kind of enjoyed myself."

"Enjoyed yourself ?" exclaimed Ed, incredulously. "You are letting all of that applause go to your head! Those people damn near killed you!"

"I didn't say I wanted to stay," said Marcus, "but the party after nearly being killed was damn good!"

"We need to get you out of there, before you get turned by them again and think it's a great idea to be one of them. Whatever they are," said Ed.

"So, you don't think they are human?" said Marcus.

"I don't think they are normal humans, I really don't. And their society is rotten and creepy. I am pretty sure, that Simon Cornish was killed by them. But, I don't know why. And, I have a feeling he is one of many," said Ed.

"Right now, I think we have a collection of 'don't knows', and a history of missing people from different parts of the country. We have nothing that would pin the good folk of Ollenberry down though. No proof at all."

"That's why I just intend to, get you and your stuff, and get the hell out of there."

"There might be a way, to get some proof," said Marcus. " Just a chance, because right now I agree we have nothing."

"What is it?" said Ed.

"Before Aubrey was attacked by those bigfoot creatures, or whatever they were, I managed to stick up a trail camera. Normally those creatures are damn elusive, and it's been conjectured that in all probability they can sense and avoid trail cameras. What if though, they were so engrossed in the attack, that they completely forgot about the cameras? That they made a mistake?"said Marcus.

"We would have the footage of the century! It wouldn't tie any missing persons to Ollenberry, but the media would be crawling all over that place for years. It would bring them international scrutiny, which they desperately want to avoid. It would stop them," said Marcus.

"I agree, that's a good plan. I don't think I am up to any climbing or trekking though," said Ed.

"You don't have to worry about that," said Marcus. "I know two local guys, Rusty and Wes, who I think will help us," then he added, "How quickly do you think you can be out of there?"

"How quickly do you think you need me?" said Ed.

"I have to play things as though they are normal," said Marcus. "Normal for this town anyway. Aubrey wants me to go to her church tomorrow. I work at Tate's the next day."

"Just shooting off with you, and missing those two days, would arouse huge suspicion, I think," said Marcus. "The following day, I know, Aubrey has arranged to go out with her kids, to the local fair. We could go then."

"I think it best to go that evening, but I could also go earlier in the day," said Marcus.

"That should work well," said Ed. "It gives me time to rest here, and then travel only in the daylight. I am hoping that cloud has given me up for dead, but I am not certain. It sure is damn persistent."

"In the meantime," said Marcus, "I will continue as normal, and try to gather as much information as I can. The church should be interesting, and maybe I can learn something while I am at the fair too. I need to understand their motivations if I am going to be able to defeat them."

"That sounds like a plan," said Ed. "Just don't enjoy yourself too much," Ed jokingly.

"I will try my best not to," Marcus replied.

"The Doctor is coming," said his nurse smiling, as she returned to his room. "Thank you," said Ed. He couldn't help but think what beautiful red hair she had.

"I don't think we should wait," said Mr. Tate. "Nobody has come this far in generations. We need to do it now."

"I agree with you," said Aubrey. "He is smart. Which is the main reason he has got so far. Plus, he must have had a bit of luck, but then so did we, and I think that's a good thing. He has friends who would stop it too, I can sense it. Once he goes through the ceremony though, he will be one of us, and our problems will disappear. It's time. How soon can you set it up?"

"Give me at least a few days," Mr. Tate replied. "I will need to make sure that all the family members are gathered together for it. In the meantime, take him to the Church, as planned. Get him ready."

" Abe has reported that the Bigfoot's sense it too. The Bigfoot's that are left, attacked a farm on the outskirts of Ollenberry yesterday. Nobody was hurt, but by all accounts, it was a close-run thing." said Mr. Tate.

We can't have them showing their faces, especially with the ceremonies going on. But, they are becoming increasingly desperate."

"I will take Marcus to the Church and prepare him," said Aubrey.

"Very good," Mr. Tate replied. "And I will let you know when we are ready to go."

Marcus was looking forward to going to the Church. Not because he was particularly religious, rather it was more about what he felt he could learn about the culture and society here. Aubrey had joked with him that he had three tests to perform.

He had soon realized that this was no joke. The first two tests had nearly killed him. He didn't want to be around for the third to take place.

He was hoping that he could get out with Ed, after they had gathered any evidence of what was going on here. At the moment though, it was important to lay low, and learn as much as he could.

In the meantime, Aubrey seemed very happy with him, which was perfect.

"Is there anything you would particularly like me to wear today?" asked Marcus.

"No," Aubrey replied, "it's all good. As long as you are smart. You are to be the guest of honor today. Preacher Harris is really looking forward to meeting you."

"What type of Church is it?" asked Marcus. "I am presuming of course that you are Christian. There is, no doubt, much more to it than that. I am sure. For example, do you believe in predestination? Do you evangelize?"

"Those are good questions," Aubrey replied. "And, from what I understand, Preacher Harris has prepared a sermon around our religion, so that you can best understand it.

We are, of course, Christians. You can be assured of that, and we do believe in predestination. We feel that people are chosen by God, to be in our Church family. We do not evangelize to others outside our area."

"What about the Clamash? They seem to keep themselves to themselves, do they evangelize?"

"Huh," said Aubrey snorting. "They are all fools. They feel bound to stay in the same historical period as their ancestors. For no good reason. They are ignorant."

"They say that they abhor technology for example, yet they will think nothing of picking and choosing that of it which they wish to use. You must have seen them at Tate's for example."

"I have," said Marcus. "They were polite but kept their distance."

"Believe me," said Aubrey, "that's a good thing. Anyway, let's go now. If you have any more questions, we can discuss them tonight, after the sermon."

"Of course," said Marcus.

The church was an unassuming red brick building, surrounded by acres of flat farmland. On the way there, Aubrey explained to Marcus that the original building had been destroyed by a fire. "It was at the same time that the town hall was destroyed, it was a tough time for our people."

"That seems a strange coincidence," said Marcus. "The buildings must be at least ten miles apart."

Marcus saw Aubrey's face darken. Then she said, "Yes, it was a bad time for our families. We faced attacks, but we overcame them."

"Attacks? Attacks from whom?" said Marcus. "Was it other settlers? Native Americans? Or raiders of some kind?"

"They were a type of raider. They wanted what we had, and we wanted what they had. It was a battle for survival. We won, and they lost. It is as simple as that," Aubrey replied.

"Do they still live in the area?" asked Marcus. "Are they connected with the modern-day families in some way?"

"Only a few remain," Aubrey replied. "Thankfully, they have almost died out now. I hope you will not meet them."

"They would only destroy you, me and everything the families have built here. That is exactly what they would do, if they are given half a chance. They are much worse than the Clamash. The Clamash resent us, but will do nothing against us, because they are afraid."

"Where do they live now?" asked Marcus. "I would love to study their culture."

"Their culture is barbaric. They live as savages," said Aubrey. "Even their appearance is frightening to behold. Believe me when I tell you, that you will find no written record of what they stand for, or believe. They seek only to obliterate what we have achieved here. That will become very clear to you when you complete the last test."

"I see," said Marcus. Trying to remain as impassive as he could. "And when will that be?"

"Very soon," Aubrey replied. "I will explain all about it when it is time. Come now though, it is time for church."

"Of course," said Marcus, smiling as he got out of the car. He would love to know more about this enemy of the families, as they might well prove to be potential allies. He could not pump Aubrey right now, for any more information on them today. He resolved to do so as soon as he could, though.

So far, he had only Ed and Katy on his side. He knew that by challenging the families, he faced a very determined and considerable enemy, who had no doubt killed many times before.

If the outside of the church was somewhat pedestrian, the interior of it was completely the reverse. Paintings adorned the walls. Not crude one's either. They were beautifully detailed canvases.

As he entered the Church, Marcus could see a painting of wagons by a small creek, with haggard looking men and women gathering wood and chopping down trees. The next painting he saw, portrayed them building homesteads.

Another painting depicted, what must have been the creation of the first streets in Ollenberry. In it, the first shops were being built. The store front of Giles's clothes shop clearly displayed.

The next painting, was more intense, with what looked like open graves. Marcus reckoned that there were at least twenty of them, placed carefully around the Church.

"They show our history," said Aubrey. "The struggles we had in the past, and they go right up until the present day."

"They are remarkable," said Marcus, "it is an amazing record of history and survival. I don't

Evil In Ollenberry

remember seeing anything like these, anywhere else."

"Thank you," said Aubrey. "We are very proud of them."

"You are lucky to have so many talented artists, over hundreds of years, in such a small community," said Marcus.

Aubrey smiled, and then she said. "Thank you, Marcus, that is very kind of you to say. There is something about this place which accentuates creativity. We have many musical people and artists, in our community."

The carpet inside the church was plush and thick. The pews were polished mahogany, on which were placed purple velvet cushions.

The Altar was at the front, on a raised platform, on which stood a carved gold and silver table. It was draped with a white linen cloth, which had a circle in the middle of it.

Marcus could see that the cloth, had a large sun on it, which shone down into a small creek. In that picture, he could see small brown figures, people presumably he thought, amidst trees.

"That is an unusual motif for a church," said Marcus. "What is the significance?"

"It is unique to our Church," said Aubrey, with an unmistakable note of pride in her voice. "It symbolizes how we had to defeat nature, to survive and be who we are."

"Defeat nature?" said Marcus. "Most religions seem to stress the importance of living in nature, yet yours emphasizes defeating it?"

"We are the highest beings," said Aubrey. "The creator made sure of that. We merely took what he offered. Preacher Harris is here now, I am sure he will explain more in his sermon."

From a small side door, near the back of the church, a tall thin man appeared. He was dressed in a white linen robe , that bore the same motif on it, as the altar. The congregation immediately stood up, and began singing in that strange language they had first heard at the cookout.

The Preacher, moved erratically, bobbing and swaying. He carried a bowl in one hand, which looked to be made of silver, and a polished wooden club in the other. He walked down the aisle slowly, taking two steps forward, before he took one step back.

Behind the Preacher, walked three small children, two girls and a boy. Marcus guessed that the children must be seven or eight years old. One carried a bowl of fruit, one a tray with cakes and bread, and one an empty bowl.

Evil In Ollenberry

When Preacher Harris reached the altar, he thrust the club into the air, before shouting "Hallelujah!" Immediately, the crowd fell silent.

"We are here today, brothers and sisters, not because of luck. Let me remind you of that." The crowd immediately, mumbled their approval at this statement.

Preacher Harris went on, "The things that we went through to survive, were terrible to behold. Starvation was the norm!"

"Our hunger, was so intense, that we were forced to eat grass from the fields. We were desperate, and we prayed that the grass we ate, would give us sustenance. We prayed to be sustained, like the beasts of the field!"

" As you know though, it did not! Yet, we were blessed by the creator, who in his almighty wisdom, brought us to this place! This wonderful place where we were able to live well, and carve out our community, from nothing! We accepted the donation from our Creator, and built on it!"

"Yes, we did!" shouted a man in the crowd.

"Now, my brothers and sisters, take of the empty bowl."

Marcus watched at the bowl, was passed from person to person in the congregation.

"If we had not accepted the bounty that was offered to us, this would have been our staple. This is what you would have had. Pain and hunger. Followed by death. Did we accept that though?"

"No!" shouted the congregation in unison.

"No! Exactly!" said Preacher," No, we did not accept that." "Now, please eat the result of that decision."

As soon as he said that, the bowl containing the fruit was passed around.

"Please take some," Aubrey whispered to him, "even if it's only a grape. Partaking is an important part of the ritual."

Marcus did as he was asked, while the preacher continued.

"Then, the plague came. Many died. The families weeped as a third of them were wiped out. We had tried to live in unison with nature, but what had it taught us?" he said.

"The Creator wanted us to know that it was a mistake for his chosen beings to behave like that, so he punished us for our stupidity. What fools we were!" He shouted.

"When the power to heal came upon us, we took it! Took it, with all the force we had. Smiting our foes! We did what we had to do!"

With that, Preacher Harris struck the altar three times with the club. In response, the congregation gave three claps of their hands.

Then he went on, "Then what were we to do my brothers and sisters? I ask you again, what were we to do?"

"Take!" The congregation shouted. "Yes, exactly, take!" returned Preacher, "And that is exactly what we did! We took! We took it from the savages who were here! We cast them aside, as we joyfully did the will of our Creator!"

"Those who did not join us, namely the Clamash, were destined to be outsiders, scratching around in their perpetual poverty," he said.

"We have been blessed to enjoyed everlasting bounty! No more disease! No more suffering! No more death! We were, and still remain, in a state of constant renewal." said Preacher Harris.

"The things we did, we did out of necessity." He professed. "We were told by the Creator, to reap the harvest. And, that is precisely what we did!"

"We have experienced such great joy, as a result. You know this, my brethren and sisters! We are pure and we are free. Now, partake of today's bounty!" shouted the Preacher, to the congregation.

The third bowl was passed around now, containing the cakes and bread. Marcus took a bite of some carrot cake. It was delicious.

"That is the best damn cake I have ever tasted", he whispered to Aubrey.

"That is because it is blessed," said Aubrey smiling. "It has been transformed , by the blessings we have been given."

"There is one among us today, who seeks to join us," Preacher Harris said. "This is a very unique situation for us. Yet, we need to remember something of utmost importance."

"Our Creator, instructed us all, on how we are to strengthen our blood. This can only happen, when we determine that a human is truly worthy. We have very stringent tests and challenges, that a human must conquer, to even be considered." said the Preacher.

"We must heed the Creator's will, if we are to maintain the bounty. The same bounty , that our families worked so hard to maintain, for us," he said.

"And, one sits amongst us today, ready soon to embark upon his 'Initiation.' Preacher Harris said, as he outstretched his right hand toward the congregation.

"Marcus, will you please come up to the altar?" Preacher Harris asked.

Initially, Marcus froze, as his mind absorbed being singled out from the church congregation. He had hoped to be quiet, to just sit near the back row of pews, and absorb the service.

Once again though, he found himself to be the center of attention. I should have known , he thought to himself.

"Don't be shy babe, go forward," said Aubrey. She prodding him forward, by pressing her finger into his stomach.

"What is going to happen?" said Marcus, the reluctance in his voice unavoidably obvious.

Aubrey gripped his hand firmly in hers, and then she shouted ,

"It seems that Marcus is shy, Preacher Harris." I will help him."

Aubrey led Marcus, firmly by his hand, to the front of the church. She led him, and then presented him to Preacher Harris. Then, Aubrey walked back, to her place within the congregation.

The Preacher, then produced a small silver bottle, from a side pocket, on his robe.

Marcus noted that the silver bottle, was ornately decorated, and had a beautiful, polished glass bottle stop. It was suspended on a silver chain, which shimmered in the sanctuary lighting.

One of the children, now stepped forward, and passed a gold plate to the preacher. On the delicate plate, there was placed a small golden cup, which was studded with rubies.

"The families knew about the importance of sacrifice. To create the world that they needed, they sacrificed their past wealth, to create sacred objects. To this very day, we still hold these objects, as most precious and sacred." said Preacher Harris, as he recounted this ancient story of the People.

The preacher now poured the contents of the vial into the golden cup, and handed it to Marcus. It looked like red wine, but lighter in color.

"Now drink," said Preacher Harris.

Marcus hesitated.

"Drink it, babe. It's actually pretty good, you will like it." said Aubrey.

Marcus put the cup to his lips and drank. The wine did indeed taste good. It was both salty and sweet, unlike any wine that he had tasted before.

Instantly, he felt remarkably energized and strong. He also felt happy! He felt so happy, that he instantly burst into laughter.

As soon as he did so, Aubrey also started to laugh, followed by the rest of the congregation. "I am sorry, I can't help it," said Marcus.

"There is no need to apologize," Aubrey replied. "Feeling joy is good now. It's exactly the right reaction."

"Now, the cleansing must take place. Sister Aubrey, please take him down to the creek," said Pastor Harris.

"Babe," said Aubrey, "you must go into the restroom. Inside, you will find a robe, that has been placed over a chair. The robe looks like the Preacher's robe. Go change into the robe."

" You must wear the robe, and nothing else. No other clothes. Do you understand ?"

"Why am I expected to do that?" said Marcus.

"It is our cleansing ceremony," said Aubrey. "The final part of you, is being accepted into the church. Its only takes a few minutes. I love you. Please do it for me."

"Of course," said, a still deliriously happy Marcus.

He emerged from the bathroom, resplendent in his robe. Aubrey then led him by the hand out of the church. The rest of the congregation followed behind, singing in their own strange language.

Preacher Harris, slowly waded deep into the creek. The Preacher, then motioned for Marcus to join him.

"Off you go now, babe," said Aubrey.

Marcus waded into the creek, until he was in water up to his waist. Finally, he stood directly in front of Preacher Harris.

"You are ready now. It is time for the cleansing." With that, Marcus could feel Preacher Harris pushing down lightly, on top of his head.

As the Preacher did so, he motioned for Marcus to drop down into the water. Marcus, dutifully did so, and found himself submerged three times.

After the third submersion, Marcus finally was able to lift his head out of the water and stand back up.

Preacher Harris spun him around, to face the crowd. Then he said, "It is done. Like the families, he has done what he had to do, and been cleansed as a result."

"All praise to the families!" shouted the congregation, in unison. "All praise to the Creator!

"Life is what we need!" They exclaimed.
"We took the bounty, and we were righteous! We
are One! Now, he is a One with us!"

Marcus waded out of the water, and
instantly felt cold. The effect that the wine had on
him, was starting to wear off, he thought.

He went into the restroom and dried
himself off, before changing back into his own
clothes. Aubrey was waiting for him outside, when
he emerged. The congregation had begun to
disperse.

"Thank you so much, for doing that for me,
babe." Aubrey said, "I can't tell you how grateful
I am to you."

"My pleasure," said Marcus. "I can't say,
that the experience wasn't very strange. But, so
are a lot of things around here, I have learned.

Aubrey laughed at this, and then she said
,"Now we need to get you home. You have a big
day at Tate's tomorrow."

When he got to Tate's the next morning,
Tara was waiting for him. This was unusual, as she
normally started her shift a couple of hours earlier
than him.

" I have been instructed, to take you
straight to Mr. Tate's office, sir," Tara said.

"Sir? Really?" said Marcus, laughing. " I think we will just carry on with first names, unless you would like me to call you `my lady`, or something!"

"I am serious," she said. "Those were my clear instructions from personnel. "Good luck Marcus." Then, just as he began heading off, she added, "and be careful."

Marcus knocked on the door to the office. The moment he did so, the door was immediately opened, by Mr. Tate himself. It was as if he had been waiting inside the door.

"Good morning, Marcus." said Mr. Tate. "Please take a seat."

"Thank you so much," said Marcus.

"Marcus, we are so very pleased with you, here at Tate's. You are now a celebrity in the town." Mr. Tate said.

"Therefore, I have decided to promote you, to deputy store manager. This is effective immediately." Mr. Tate said.

"You will report only to me, from now on. After this briefing, I will take you to your new office." said Mr. Tate.

"Really?" said Marcus, who was astonished by what he had just heard.

"I have only been here just a few days. I thank you, but I don't feel worthy of such a promotion." Marcus said. "I am sure there are people, who have been here a lot longer than I have. Employees, who are much more worthy than I. I am just happy, to be doing my job with Tara."

"The families discussed it last night, after your anointment into the Church. It is what we all desire. So, it will be happening. Unless you choose to refuse." said Mr. Tate.

"I choose to say yes!" said Marcus." Thank you so much."

Now, Mr. Tate led Marcus out to the storefront. Much to his surprise, Marcus could see that all of the employees, were already lined up waiting for him.

"I am pleased to say, that Marcus has accepted his new position. I know that many of you were involved, in encouraging me to make this move. No doubt, he understands that there will be a lot for him to learn." said Mr. Tate.

"With his ability, to 'Blue Sky' think though, I have no doubt that he will be a success! If in doubt, what do we say at Tate's?" Mr. Tate asked the crowd.

"Suck it and see!" Shouted the crowd.

Mr. Tate turned to Marcus and said, "Let me show you to your new office now. I thought, that I would give you today, to adjust to it."

"Marcus, I know you are off tomorrow, and there won't be many duties for a few days anyway." Mr. Tate said. "Also, I must adjust the management structure, and allocate you some of my departments to run. So, enjoy settling in."

Mr. Tate walked down the corridor which led to his office, while Marcus followed behind him.

Mr. Tate turned a sharp right, just before he got to his own office. He opened a door, which already had a brass name plate on the outside. The name plate was engraved with the name 'Marcus.

"Here is your new office," said Mr. Tate. "Enjoy it."

The room was dimly lit, just like Mr. Tate's. Marcus, now found that he liked the dimness of his office. The dimness, was comfortable seemed to suit his eyes much better.

In the middle of his office, was a huge wooden desk. A green leather armchair was placed in the corner. Bookshelves were lined up around the walls.

A large rug with the same motif, that he had seen in the Church, dominated the hardwood floor. All in all, it looked much like a nineteenth century parlor.

"Do you like it?" said Mr. Tate.

"It's perfect, "said Marcus. "Thank you so much."

"Very good," said Mr. Tate. "I will see you soon."

Marcus waited until he had heard Mr. Tate's footsteps fading. Then he began exploring the room. It was clearly bizarre that he had been promoted so quickly, but then everything about Ollenberry was bizarre.

He decided to look through the bookshelves, to see if he could get some more information. But, the books there offered few clues, as most of them were farming and hardware related   .

On the left-hand side of the office was a small white wooden door. He hadn't noticed it when he first came in, as the lighting was so dim. He tried the door, but it was locked. Where might the key be?

He looked for it in his new desk, but to no avail. Damn, he thought to himself. He tried to look through the keyhole of the door but could see only darkness on the other side.

Evil In Ollenberry

He paced around the room, looking for anything else that might help him. It would be a long day in this room with nothing to do, he thought. Maybe he would just force the white door open. He tried slamming his weight against it, but it remained stuck.

The only way he could get through it without the key was by kicking it in, and the noise this created would inevitably bring the entire staff of Tate's down on him.

Then it struck him. What was unusual about this room? Everything was normal, if dated furniture. All that is, except the rug.

He rushed over to the rug and pulled it up. And, there it was. A trapdoor built into the floor! Excitedly, he pulled the brass handle on it, and pulled it open.

He saw steps leading down into the darkness. At first, his heart sunk as he had no flashlight with him. Then he realized that there was a simple light switch on the wall, only a few steps down.

He wondered if he should cover up the entrance before he left, and just slip out sneakily. He quickly dismissed this idea though. He had no idea where he was going. If he got trapped down there, nobody would know. At least if he left the trapdoor open he reasoned , and he did get trapped , then people would come looking for him. After all, nobody had said that he couldn't go down here.

The steps led down to a long and empty narrow corridor, with brick whitewashed walls on either side of it. The corridor was well lit , but Marcus walked slowly , listening for sound. There was nothing. He continued on, following the corridor, as it continued in a straight line. It seemed endless. There was nothing but silence. By then, he had been walking for at least ten minutes. He was thinking of turning back, when he saw that the corridor came to an abrupt end, just thirty feet in front of him.

There were steps and a trapdoor. Cautiously, he climbed the steps and pushed open the door above his head. He was in a room, which was, like the study adorned with bookshelves. There was only one door in this room, and hearing muffled sound behind it, he crept slowly up to the room. Marcus , then he listened to the conversation on the other side of it.

"Yes of course, we can reserve that for you. We will let you have it this afternoon." He instantly recognized the voice. It was the librarian!

This door led to the secret room that Aubrey had gone in to, when they were at the library. He was in the library! This was one place he was forbidden from entering. He knew he hadn't much time

Evil In Ollenberry

He quickly turning around, he looked at the books which were piled haphazardly on a table in front of him. He had only caught a brief glimpse of it. But, one of the books looked familiar to him.

Marcus, thought he had seen Aubrey, reading that very book. The day at the library, and she had entered the 'private' room, and asked him to wait outside.

He considered taking the book, but quickly dismissed the idea. If that book was found to be missing, it wouldn't be hard to trace his movements back through the trapdoor.

The librarians must know that it exists, he reasoned. After all, unlike the one in his office, it wasn't even covered by a rug. Quickly, he flicked through the book. He was taking pictures, as quickly as he could with his phone. He only managed to get a few photos, and he then heard voices getting nearer to the door.

Then he shut the book, and descended the steps as quickly as he could. He slid the trapdoor closed carefully behind him. He was just in time, as he heard the librarian. She must be with another person, judging by the multiple footfalls.

"Ah, yes of course, it is here," said the librarian." It is here. I imagine you need it for the ceremony."

"Yes," said the other woman, "I need to scrutinize it carefully."

Marcus frowned. He thought he had heard that voice before somewhere, but he couldn't be sure.

"I am sure you have all the details in the book memorized by now," said the librarian.

"We have not conducted a full ceremony like this for nearly two hundred years." said the other woman sharply. "Details are important."

"Of course," said the librarian, submissively, before shutting the door.

Marcus was astonished. He knew who the other woman was now. He had only heard her speak in that strange local language before, that was why, it had taken a long time for him to process . It was the healing woman, Elsie! She was speaking to the librarian in English!

He continued to listen for a few minutes more, but there was nothing but silence. Fearing that he might be eventually missed, he went back down the corridor to his office. Marcus entered his dimly lit office, and shut the door behind him.

As soon as he sat down, he began looking through the photos he had taken of the book. The pages were mainly inscribed with words derived from the local language. At first, he struggled to comprehend anything from the writings.

But, there were some Latin words, which he understood to a level. By piecing together the Latin words, along with the sketched illustrations, Marcus gradually gained insight into the meaning of the pages.

He was confident, that he was correct in his instinctive interpretation. This definitely appeared to be some form of spell book.

There was a picture of a woman grinding, what looked like herbs, with a pestle and mortar. There was also, a picture of the same woman, opening her arms and calling out incantations.

Strangely, she seemed to be holding a giant bone in her hand. It was the last picture though, that drew his particular attention.

Here, unmistakably, was a picture if what looked like a Bigfoot. The same woman, who was clearly a witch, was pointing at the Bigfoot. Most likely, mumbling some sort of spell as she did so, Marcus guessed.

A man had joined her, in the next picture. The man seemed to be jumping, while he held a staff or club above his head. In the picture it looked like, he was about to bring down the big club on the Bigfoot's head.

This is amazing! I wish I had time to decipher this, he thought out loud. At least though, I will be able to show it to Ed, Rusty and Wes tomorrow, when I meet up with them.

This finding certainly didn't surprise him. It seemed obvious to him, that the people of Ollenberry, were indulging in a malevolent form of Witchcraft.

The ceremony he had attended, at the town's church, seemed to have nothing to do with Christianity, whatsoever.

Also, the attacks on Aubrey made sense now. Now, he understood what had happened at the Fort. The Bigfoots hadn't sought to bother with him at all, rather they had focused their energies entirely on Aubrey!

He was only targeted, because he was with Aubrey. When he and Aubrey were running to her car, the Bigfoots, must have been trying to get to Aubrey, not him. Yet, Marcus had a question, still unanswered.

Where did Katy fit into all of this?

Katy, clearly had some magical gifts. Indeed, without her, he would almost certainly be dead by now. Yet, she seemed to use her magic to help, not harm.

Marcus spent the rest of the day wrapped up in thought. Nobody knocked on his door, nobody called him. When it reached exactly five o' clock, he slipped out of his office.

"Enter," said Mr. Tate, in response to the knock on his door.

"He went for it," said Tara. "We watched it all on the hidden cameras."

"Excellent," said Mr. Tate.

"Yes, I would agree," said Tara. "There was one point, which I thought I should raise. He took some photos of the spellbook, with his phone."

"It's of no real consequence," said Mr. Tate. "The ceremony is less than forty-eight hours away. If he joins us, then he will destroy them."

"If he join us doesn't, then we will destroy them. If he shares them, we will say it is a 'photoshop,' and laugh." He said.

"Nobody will believe it. That is one of the reasons we have kept so safe, for so long." he said.

"I still think it's a risk, letting him go to them," said Tara. "And he will have his friends with him too."

"I would agree with you on that," said Mr. Tate." I think though, it's the best way we can draw them in. Let those creatures think they have a chance, and then we will destroy them."

Tara nodded, and then she said, "it will be a good harvest."

"A great harvest!" said Mr. Tate, thumping his fist hard on the table as he did so.

CHAPTER SEVEN

-There Is No Such Thing As Fate-

Marcus had arranged to meet Ed about half a mile from Aubrey's house, by a small stretch of woodland next to an abandoned house.

Ed was exactly on time! And, for the first time in ages, Marcus felt relief, as he saw his friend's car approaching.

"Please tell me I am not crazy," said Marcus, as they drove to the Fort.

"Listen buddy, I would have not said you were crazy, even if I had just heard your story alone, without proof. And remember, I have had that damn cloud attack me twice now!" said Ed.

"The images from that spell book you just showed me, only add to it. Whatever the hell is going on here, seems rotten to me. We need to stop it, and stop it now." Ed said.

"I am glad Rusty and Wes will be with us," said Marcus. "They should give us some good support. We don't know them, but I am going to take a risk by telling them everything. We will need their help if we are going to get that camera. I don't think you are in any condition to make the climb, after just being in hospital."

"I want to disagree with you, but I can't." said Ed. "If you have to move rapidly, and you almost certainly will, then I will just slow you down. As a consequence, I would be putting everyone at risk."

"I agree," said Marcus. "Let's hope they believe our story, and don't just turn their car around. Otherwise, I am in for a rough time."

When they got to the hill, Rusty and Wes were already waiting for them. Both of them were holding shotguns, and they looked tense when Marcus and Ed got out of the car.

"I have a very strange story to tell you, gentlemen. You are either going to believe it all, or think I am insane." said Marcus.

"Do your worst," said Rusty." We are all ears."

"I agree," said Wes." Just tell it like it is."

Marcus nodded, and then proceeded to tell them his entire story. He began, with when he found the note with the name Simon Cornish on it. He explained, that Ed had then confirmed that Cornish had mysteriously disappeared.

Marcus relayed intricate details, of the strange events at the shops, including his first encounter with Katy. To the best of his ability, he sought to include every important detail.

He wrapped up, by telling them what had happened at Tate's yesterday. As the final piece of evidence, he produced the photos he had taken of the spell book. The spell book, he had found in the 'secret room' in the town's library.

"I didn't know the depth of it," said Rusty, "or the connection with Bigfoot, but I am not surprised by it. Wes here, has been doing some digging for a while."

"Yes", said Wes," there have been rumors that the `families` of Ollenberry, are not what they seem. Rumors, going back generations in the surrounding towns. Even now, a lot of people are wary about coming here after dark. I had always dismissed them as old wives tale's until I saw a few photos in the county museum one day. There aren't many photos of them, they must avoid having them taken if they possibly can, but there are enough. There is a photo of what looks like

Aubrey and Mr. Tate from one hundred years ago. Then there is another one taken ten years ago. They are unmistakably the same people. Far beyond family resemblance.

"Yes," said Marcus, "I saw the same set of photos in Ollenberry library I think."

"How do they keep it going though," said Ed? " I mean they have to resgister births and deaths?"

"That's a good question," said Wes. "And I think the answer is corruption. The mayor is always a member of one of the families, the Sheriff too. They falsify records. Shift around. Mother becomes youngest cousin for example. Even in this day and age, with a pool of a few hundred people, it isn't that difficult to do. Newcomers do come to town and have kids, and that will mask it too. Even so, the only clue is the birthrate. For Ollenberry given its size, it is abnormally low. Other than that, there is nothing that would lead you to imagine there was anything abnormal about it."

"Crime here is low. They are working hard to keep out of the public eye. They are evil though, no doubt about it. Whatever they have done to keep themselves alive, cannot be good. I have been after information on them for years, and you have added extra pieces to the puzzle. And I thank you for that,"said Wes.

Evil In Ollenberry

"You are very welcome," said Marcus.

"The Bigfoot connection is a big surprise to us," though said Rusty. "I cannot think what they are up to with them. The only good thing to come out of all this is that it is both amazing and wonderful to know that they really do exist."

"They certainly do," Marcus replied ."I have seen them with my own eyes. Yet in the book, the families seem to be persecuting them for some reason. Do you have any idea why they would do so?"

"I can't think of any," said Rusty.

" As far as I understand it, the only thing the families have ever been interested in, is self-preservation, at all costs. They must be emphatic about that, it has kept them together for hundreds of years. Maybe the Bigfoot attacked them in some way? I don't know. I wish we had more time to prepare. I know whatever cermony they have for you is planned to happen in just a few days , so we have to be ready with what we have got. Maybe the Bigfoots will come out again when we go and get the trail cameras." Rusty said.

"If they do, I hope they don't mistake us for one of the family members." Said Marcus, "after all they have seen me with Aubrey."

"I really hope it doesn't come to it,"said Wes. "We are ready if we need to be though."

Evil In Ollenberry

Leaving Ed by the car, Marcus, Wes and Rusty began climbing up the trail . Marcus noted again that the forest around them was quiet. It felt like something was listening. Eventually, they came to the place where they had to turn off the trail, to climb towards the Fort.

As soon as he did so, Marcus felt that heavy feeling in his body which he was familiar with from the first time he came here, only this time it was worse. Feeling breathless, he turned and looked at both Wes and Rusty, who were flanking him. He could see that both of them were going slowly, but they seemed to be having nothing like the difficulty that he was having.

"I know you are struggling," said Wes" we are nearly there. Just another minute more though, and you will make it. Or I can get the trail camera down for you, if you like?"

"I will make it," said Marcus, almost breathlessly.

By the time he got to the top, Marcus was so exhausted that he could barely stand. He felt like he had been climbing in Nepal, rather than going up a hill that couldn't have been more than three or four hundred feet high. He could barely see through the sweat that was dripping into his eyes, as he began to unstrap the camera.

"You will wait there and tell your friends to lower their weapons, if you do not want to die." A voice, deep and resonant, was speaking loudly to him. He spun around in all directions, but there was nobody around but Wes and Rusty.

"Did you hear that?" Marcus said.

"What?" said Wes, in response. "I heard nothing."

"Me neither." said Rusty.

"Tell your friends to put their weapons down now!" Said the voice. It sounded so deep, not human, yet it was unmistakably speaking English.

"It's a voice," said Marcus." Deep, speaking English. It is saying that you must put your weapons down. I am amazed you can't hear it."

"I know exactly what it is," said Wes. "It is one of the Bigfoots. There are some accounts of certain people having the ability to communicate with them. I had previously dismissed them as being from people with vivid imaginations. Some might have been true though."

"I agree, and I vote that we just put our guns down, really slowly. If we can't see them, and they can see us, we are going to have little chance if they do decide to attack us, and from what you said there are seven of them around here," said Rusty.

"We are doing as you ask," said Marcus.

Wes and Rusty then slowly put their rifles on the ground. After that, they added their two pistols.

It was then that they emerged. Marcus recognized them instantly. They were the two creatures that had attacked Aubrey, when he had first come to the fort. The white one, stood around seven feet tall, while the black one stood around six feet, five. Both had saggital crests, and a wide flat nose. They rippled with muscle. As far as Marcus could see they were exactly the same, with one important difference. The black one, was obviously a female, having round and pendulous breasts.

"Your friends will not understand our conversation, but you can translate for them," said the white one. It watched him carefully as it spoke. Marcus got the impression that if he made any sudden movements, he would regret it.

"It says that you will not be able to understand it," Marcus said.   " I can though, and I will translate for you."

'Thanks" said Wes. "It sounds like some sort of Asiatic language to me." "We will just listen to you. I feel astonished and privileged right now, I do not feel threatened."

"I agree," said Rusty.

" I am going to explain what has happened to you now, and the history of this place,"said the white creature." Some of it will no doubt be uncomfortable to you. First of all though, please do not refer to me as `it`. I am called Hockran, and I am the leader of my clan. And this is Neestra."

"Pleased to meet you", Marcus replied. "I am Marcus, and this is Wes and Rusty."

"Very good," said Hockran." I do not know what brought you here, but I am guessing that you were encouraged to come by one of the family members, is that correct?"

"It is," said Marcus. "You saw her on that day you attacked us, her name is Aubrey."

"Yes, I am familiar with her." Said Hockran. "We all are."

"Firstly, the families are not what they seem, as I am sure you know by now. None of them have died for hundreds of your years. They are twisted things. They have gone against the natural order of the world. They have undoubtedly killed anyone who sought to reveal who they are, and anyone who did not live up to their expectations. The fact that you have got as far as you have, is remarkable in itself."Hockran said.

"I had a lot of help," said Marcus. " I will be happy to tell you my story later, but do please continue."

"When the human settlers first came to our valley," said Hockran, "we were not unduly worried. We were familiar with what you call Native Americans. They did not bother us, and we did not bother them."

"However, we quickly learned that these people were not like the Native Americans. They tore the land up, and guarded it with dogs, so that travel between our clans became very difficult. Still, we were prepared to do our best to avoid these new people, and get on with our lives." said Hockran.

"Then, one day, one of the family members, the one called Abe, shot one of us while hunting. He brought the body back to his camp, and the so-called healing woman Elsie. She is in reality a gifted and dark witch, made potions from the dead body. We do not understand all of what she did of course, but it must have given them strength and speed, because now they became not only at least as strong as us, but they also became extremely quick." Said Hockran.

" They then took it upon themselves to persecute us whenever they could. Finally, the plague started to take them, as nothing else would. You will have to forgive me, but we really did rejoice at this point, because we thought that they might finally leave, and that we would be at peace."

" We were wrong though. Despite our own magic, which you experienced on the way up here, they hunted us down to here, our final stronghold, and nearly destroyed us all. Only a few of us escaped."

"I am very sorry," said Marcus.

"It is not your fault, said Hockran. " They take what they want, and they do not care what the consequences are. After the massacre, they took all our bodies for medicine. They healed, and as far as we know they are now immune from disease. They never die, and they never grow old."

"Do forgive me, but why have you not left?" Said Marcus. "You could go far away. Maybe join up with others of your kind, and form an alliance against them?"

"We wish we could, believe me," Hockran replied. "We are trapped here though. We are aware there are others, but we cannot leave. They have created some sort of boundary thirty miles outside of Ollenberry which we cannot pass through. Nor can we age. So, we are stuck here as we are."

"I do understand that, I experienced that particular magic myself, but on a much smaller scale." Said Marcus."When I tried to escape from Aubrey, some sort of barrier prevented me from doing so."

Hockran nodded. "They have magic we cannot fathom. Some of it is created from the very flesh of my people, but some comes from a dark and evil place. From that creature called Elsie. It is not of this earth. Now, do please tell us your story."

Marcus began with the story of how he felt he had been followed on the journey here, and how he and Ed had been attacked by the black cloud. He carried on talking about all that had happened to him since he reached Ollenberry , until the point where he had met up with Hockran and Neestra.

"Well, that explains one thing at least," said Hockran, "but we had guessed it. I am afraid you are not going to like it though."

"What is it?" Said Marcus.

" The liquid you drank in their church. It was not wine. It was blood. Our blood. It was imbued with magic. That is why you have a connection with us. That is why you can understand us when we speak."

Marcus felt his throat thicken with bile. Then he said "I am amazed and disgusted! I am truly sorry."

"It is not your fault, you had no idea." Said Hockran.

"How can we stop them though? And what do they want ot me?"

Hockran said, "I would have answered the first question by saying we have very little chance of stopping them. That is until you told me about the one you call `Katy`."

"The One called Katy, I have never heard of her before. It sounds like she has enormous power too, but not in an evil way like Elsie. She is certainly an asset."

" I cannot say what they want you for, but they seem to have gone to a lot of trouble to get you, and so there must be something to it. It seems like whatever they plan to do is in a couple of nights time."

" They must be taking you to the Dragon's mound, it is a sacred place, imbued with great power. We will help you."

" In the meantime, contact this Katy and ask her to help. We will contact the Clamash, we know some of their Elders, and we can speak in each others tongue. I think the only way we can beat them is if we join forces together."

"That sounds like a good plan", said Marcus. "How will I be able to contact you though?"

"It will be easy for you from now on. Just imagine a picture of me in your head," said Hockran. "Then speak. I will answer."

"Very good," said Marcus.

He watched then as Hockran and Neestra left, waving goodbyes before they melted into the forest.

" That was the most incredible thing I have ever seen in my life," said Rusty.

"I would have to agree, said Wes. It was amazing! And I have no clue, what any of you said."

Marcus laughed at this. "Well don't be under any illusion that I am any great prophet. The story of why I can speak to them is both horrifying and macabre. I will explain it all when we get down to Ed."

After Marcus had gone through the plan with them all, Ed said , "the key then is a coordinated attack by us , the one called Katy, the Bigfoots and the Clamash, at this Dragon mound in a few days time?"

"That is correct," said Marcus. "I will have to go through with this final test, whatever it is. Please pull me out as soon as it starts if you possibly can. I don't need to remind you how close I have come to dying in the first two."

"Of course," said Ed. "We have got your back."

"Thank you all three of you," said Marcus. "As soon as I can confirm the night of the ceremony to you, I will text you. In the meantime, I have to leave now. Aubrey will be coming to pick me up from her house soon to take me to the County Fair. Her and her kids have been there all day, but she has said she also wants to show me it. If I don't leave now, I won't be back in time, and the plan will be ruined."

Marcus and Ed exchanged some quick goodbyes with Rusty and Ed before they drove off. Marcus flew out of Ed's car when they got to the old farmhouse, and then he sprinted across the fields to Aubrey's house. He made it back, just as her car began turning into the driveway.

The fair was more fun than he expected it to be. There were food stalls, which offered gargantuan portions of mostly fried foods, agricultural stalls, where prize livestock and vegetables were displayed, and fairground rides. Marcus and Aubrey focused mainly on the rides. Most of them were for children, but there were a few that he and Aubrey could go on, and he particularly enjoyed a giant spinning wheel that used gravity to pin you to its sides as you hurled around inside it. Not long after that, and once the contents of his stomach had settled, he suggested to Aubrey that they get some food.

They sat on open benches devouring it. Aubrey managed to consume hers within almost a minute flat it seemed, while he had barely touched his burger. Then, Aubrey put down her stripped Turkey bone and said, "you are settling in very well in Ollenberry, don't you think? We are good, and you now have a great job. You have done very well."

"I think so," said Marcus. "I am ready for this final test, now. Can you tell me when it will be?"

Aubrey laughed, and then said. "I knew you were waiting to ask me that! It will be the day after tomorrow, in the evening. Tomorrow, I will take you shopping again, to pick three items from the shops just like you did before. Then, on the night of the ceremony, all the families will meet at the dragon's mound. Once it is over, after you have passed, you will be officially one of us."

"And what if I fail?" Said Marcus.

"You won't fail babe," said Aubrey, " and even if you do, I will still have always loved you, no matter what. You are very special indeed to get this far."

The phrase that Aubrey used ` will still have always loved you`, was not lost on Marcus. He decided not to press that point though. He knew only too well what would happen to him if he failed.

"You mentioned a ceremony, what is that?" said Marcus.

"Oh, wait and see," said Aubrey. "You know I enjoy giving you surprises. This will be a great one, I promise. Anyway, it will all unfold as it should do." Now she stood up and said, "do you mind if I got to the bathroom and wash my hands before we go? My hands are greasy from that turkey leg."

"Not at all," said Marcus. "I will just sit here and finish off my burger."

He waited until Aubrey was a safe distance away, and then he said "Katy come get me, Katy come get me, Katy come get me."

"I am behind you," said Katy. "Don't look round at me though. And finish your burger, it needs to be gone before she gets back. She will be suspicious otherwise, and you are always carefully watched."

"I understand, "said Marcus. "And you were right, I am going to the shops tomorrow, and the ceremony is in the night after tomorrow."

"Very good. The ceremony won't start until at least 10 pm. There is a small patch of woodland about a quarter of a mile from the dragon's mound. Tell your friends that I will meet them there at 9pm,so that we can prepare, and plan our assault. I know you will contact the Bigfoot, and they in turn will contact the Clamash. Do not worry about us, we will do everything we can to support you." Said Katy.

"How will I know when you are going to attack?" Said Marcus.

"You won't," said Katy. " Nothing is known about the ceremony you are about to undergo, but I will move on them when they are at their weakest, you can trust me on that."

"I know I can and thank you." Said Marcus.

"Just one more thing though," said Katy. "When you go to the shops tomorrow, be unpredictable. Don't pick what Aubrey expects, and don't show her what you have chosen. The families always have the initiative with their surprises. Give one to them."

"Good idea," said Marcus. "I will."

"See you soon," said Katy. Marcus kept his eyes focused firmly on his burger, but he knew she had gone . Next, he sent texts to Ed, Wes and Rusty , telling them the rendezvous time and place that they were to meet with Katy.

He felt the hardest part would be to communicate with the Bigfoot. He closed his eyes though, and firstly imagined Hockran, the bigfoot. Then, in his mind, spoke out the location and time of the meet up.

To his surprise, he was met with an almost instant reply. "I understand. we, and the Clamash will be ready."

"Wow that burger must be good," said Aubrey. "It has made you close your damn eyes when you are eating it."

"It really is," said Marcus, trying to not look too startled as he spoke. "It is delicious! I am ready to go now though, if that's okay with you?"

"Absolutely," said Aubrey. "After all, you have another big day tomorrow."

Aubrey dropped Marcus off at the shops, at around noon the next day. He was hungry, and his eyes naturally gravitated towards the sweetshop. He didn't doubt that Marion's sweets were delicious, or that they were effective, but he had decided that he wasn't going to go in there.

He wanted to do something unexpected. And, he only had three choices. He would start, he thought with Giles's clothes shop. What clothing he chose there, would determine which of the other shops he visited, he decided.

As soon as he opened the door, the little man bobbed up. He shot a beaming smile across his face.
"So good to see you, sir!" said Giles. "And I am delighted you came back!"

Marcus said, "Well, I am really happy to see you too, Giles!" Then he noticed the massive bruise across the right-hand side of his face. It was black in the center, and a livid yellow at the edges. His eyelid was swollen so much that he could barely see out of it.

"What happened to you, Giles?" said Marcus.

"Somebody thinks I talk too much," said Giles. "Let me tell you though, that is not going to stop me today."

"I really appreciate you," said Marcus softly. "And I will do my best, I promise you."

Giles simply nodded, and then moved towards the clothes racks.

"Anyway Giles," said Marcus as he followed behind him. "As I walked in here, I decided I knew exactly what I wanted."

"And what is that?" asked Giles.

"I want the suit of armor," Marcus replied." I think I am going to see some fighting tomorrow night."

"Oh, what an excellent choice!" said Giles, clapping his hands together as he did so." I am so happy! Wearing armor is nothing like it is depicted in the movies to be. For a broad and strong man like yourself, it is surprisingly lightweight. Actually, this armor, is even more lightweight, as it was fashioned by an Italian master craftsman. Come now, I will help you put it on."

Marcus was delighted when he got into the armor, he could move with ease, even run in it, should he need to.

"I think that there could be a lot of guns at my final test. Many people there will have much more experience with guns, than I have, so I decided to level things out a bit." said Marcus.

"I love your reasoning sir, and you are correct, said Giles. "The armor will withstand most bullets. They will be amazed at your choice."

"Now, I need a sword," said Marcus.

"May I be so bold as to suggest another alternative?" said Giles. "The war hammer is an excellent alternative, and I believe you will be very pleased with the results."

He went to a wall at the back of his shop, and took down from the wall, a war hammer. It looked malevolent. It was a long metal pole with a wrought iron black head. On one side of the head, there was a hammer, while on the other side of it , there protruded a wicked metal spike. Another spike jutted out from the top of it.

"The sword is a classic weapon of course, and I would expect someone who is unfamiliar with medieval weapons to choose it." Giles said.

"In reality though, it is nowhere near as effective a weapon in combat with knights , as this one. The sword can break, and a swipe from it will not cut through the armor you are wearing right now. Your enemy must to stab you to win. You however, can batter him down with this, making every blow count. Then pierce through his armor with the spike, to finish him off."

"That sounds perfect then," said Marcus, "I will take the war hammer, Giles, just as you suggested."

"You won't regret it sir, I promise you that."

"May I also add some free gifts sir, sacks to put your armor in?" said Giles.

"Giles," said Marcus, " I think you know what I am going to face during this final test don't you? And they beat you for giving what they considered too much advice to help me last time, didn't they?"

"Yes," said Giles, " and I have no doubt that they will beat me again, just like they beat Marion and Emily. I don't care though, this is a chance to be free from slavery."

"From slavery?" asked Marcus.

"I cannot tell you about that. If I do, it is not just me that would suffer as a result. I can tell you this though. You will not be able to keep this suit of armor a secret from Aubrey. You do not have to tell her, what your weapon of choice is though. I will wrap it, and place it into the sack, so she will think it is a sword. You do not have to tell her what else you have chosen. Keep it a secret. And, remember what you have already been through, and what you have learned."

Marcus was very grateful to the little shopkeeper, who had obviously shown enormous courage. Unlike the first time when he had visited the shops, Aubrey had not put him on a time limit. Today, he had plenty of time to ruminate on his final two choices. Then, his next choice came to him. Of course, it was obvious!

"I want a pig's leg, and three steaks. The biggest you have! "said Marcus.

"Of course sir!" said the ruddy faced, round little butcher. His smile was topped by an immaculately waxed moustache. "You must be having quite the party! And, can I also interest you in a chicken?" said the butcher. "They are excellent for throwing." He winked as he said this.

The butcher was on to him, thought Marcus. "I will take one of those too," said Marcus, whisking one up, and popping it into the sack.

He stepped out of the Butcher shop, and now he thought very carefully. Yes, his purchase at

the Butcher shop, the families could possibly guess
.

So, his final choice had to be really
unpredictable. Not the Antique shop this time.

Nor, Car Repair Shops or Travel Agencies.
Choosing, either of those shops to visit, might
have bought him a way out of the town. If, he had
thought about that carefully, since his first trip to
town. However, it was too late now, for he was in
it until the end.

This ceremony was a chance to stop all the
evil and death, that had been going on in
Ollenberry for centuries. That was what he wanted
more than anything . So, he was either walking out
of here as the victor, or he was a dead man.

That left the mirror shop. He hoped they
wouldn't expect that.

The door creaked reluctantly open, as he
walked in awkwardly, carrying his sacks.
Immediately, a tall, thin and wiry girl with green
hair shot up from behind the counter. She was
wide eyed, and the look on her face suggested
that she was astonished by his presence.

"Hello sir," she stammered. "I wasn't
expecting you. Nobody has ever come in here."

Marcus was banking on that fact! And,he
was hoping to catch her off guard.

"What is your best magical mirror?" He asked.

"I can't tell you best," she said, nervously. "I can make a few suggestions though."

"Please do," Marcus replied.

"Well, you will need a handheld mirror, given that I expect you need to move fast. The big one's are no use to you. We have three hand held mirrors," she said, pointing to three oval shaped mirrors on the countertop in front of her.

"The one with the wooden handle, will blind anyone you shine it at. The one with the silver handle, will reflect a vision to people of how they really are, of how their soul is. And, the one with the gold handle will make you invisible for awhile, as long as you point it at yourself."

"I will take the silver one," said Marcus.

"A cultured choice," said the young woman. As she smiled, Marcus could see that she was missing nearly half her teeth. The rest were a brilliant white.

"What did you get?" said Aubrey excitedly, when he returned to the car. "No wait, let me guess. Well, it's obvious that you got a suit of armor and a sword. And, I can smell the meat. Good choice. So, I am guessing that you got some sweets too."

"That will remain a surprise," said Marcus. "I know you like surprises."

Marcus saw just a flicker of irritation pass Aubrey's face, which she quickly suppressed. Then, she said, "Of course my love. I shall look forward to it."

That night, Aubrey pulled him into bed, stripped off his clothes and rode him. She squeezed her hands tightly around his neck, which surprised him. As he struggled for air, and writhed against the steady pressure, he felt her climax.

Marcus, caught a flash of red in her eyes, as she flung herself off of his body. Before it could truly repulse him, she was gone.

CHAPTER EIGHT

-And Now To Battle-

Aubrey had finished strapping him into his armor. It was night now, and he had been pacing about the house, and the garden. He moved his arms as rapidly as he could now, twirling them around, looking for any points which may make it stick, when he had to fight.

"Are you ready?" said Aubrey. "I think if you do any more moving around, you will tire yourself out, and you need your energy for the test."

"I am ready," Marcus replied.

"Great!"Said Aubrey. "I will drop you off at the bottom of the Dragon's mound. The test is relatively simple. What you have to do, is make it to the top of the mound. I will be waiting for you there."

"I understand," said Marcus.

The drive over was almost in silence. Even Aubrey, who was normally so upbeat, seemed tense. For a lot of it, Marcus closed his eyes, and focused. The next hour would decide not only his fate, but that of hundreds of others too.

They pulled up to the entrance to the mound, and Marcus got out of the car silently. His hands were shaking. He needed to control that, he thought.

"Wait here a few minutes. When you hear the horn sound, start your way up. I will see you at the top, my love." said Aubrey.

Marcus grunted a response and watched her drive away. Then, he unwrapped the sack containing his war hammer. He held it tightly, in his right hand. In his left hand, he held the sack with the meat in it.

Evil In Ollenberry

Now, he listened. All of the family members must be waiting here within just a few hundred feet of him, yet there was nothing but silence.

He wondered when his friends would join him in the attack. He would just have to trust their judgement.

He stepped forward, and began his ascent up the Dragon's mound. The moment he did so, he heard it. A low growl. It sounded just like the bear. It was exactly what he expected. He sighed with relief, even though he was now expecting an imminent attack.

He unwrapped the meat and carefully, placed the steaks in a line in front of him before stepping back. He was guessing about what to do next. But, at this point all he could do was guess.

This time, the creature didn't rush him. It just stared, debating whether to attack him first or devour the meat. It was thin with straggly fur, and it seemed to have cuts all over its body. It snarled at him now, exposing yellow broken fangs. It must be in pain to suffer that mouth, Marcus thought.

As it turned towards the first steak, he could see that although it had the head of a bear, its body was smaller, like that of a wolf. He had never seen anything like it. He suspected it was some creation of evil, a perversion of nature. Marcus felt sorry for the creature, in its pitiful condition, and he hoped not to have to fight it or kill it.

Slowly, he made his way up the mound, away from it, working backwards as he did so, while carefully watching it. At first, it seemed to do nothing, and Marcus was relieved. Then suddenly it screamed and began bounding straight at him!

Marcus hurled the meat in the air, and as he did so, the creature turned in mid- air to watch it.

Marcus, at that moment, thrust his war hammer upwards, piercing the creature in its side. Marcus, crouched down now, and watched as the injured animal missed him, shooting straight over his head. At first, it tried to rise up, but his legs quickly gave way, and it finally tumbled to the ground, silently.

Marcus suspected that the poor, wretched thing would be glad it was dead. He carried on silently up the mound. Moving towards the outline of what looked like a man, only a hundred feet above him.

"Well, you made short work of that there creature of ours, but I reckoned that you would," shouted the figure.

Marcus instantly recognized the voice. It was Abe.

Evil In Ollenberry

"And I was expecting you too," Marcus replied.

"I reckoned you were too," said the figure as it shuffled clumsily forward. It was Abe.

"You know," said Abe, "I wished we had just stuck to guns. No matter though, I can still stick you with this here sword."

With that, he ran forward towards Marcus, swinging his sword above his head as he did so.

Marcus jumped out of his way with ease though, and swung around to face Abe, who had now fallen to his knees with the effort.

"The thing is though Abe, you would have defeated me with a gun, no question. However, I am stronger and heavier than you, and that makes me quicker. Now, I have the edge."

Abe was breathing hard now, but sheer determination got him to his feet. His legs wobbled slightly, as he raised his sword again. Grabbing the sword with two hands, he lifted it above his head, intending to smash it down straight onto Marcus's head.

Marcus parried the blow, and pushed a grunting Abe back with his war hammer. Abe resisted, trying desperately to keep his balance as Marcus dug in with his heels.

"I guess we could call it a draw," spat Abe. "We can go on up there together If you wish."

"I don't think so," replied Marcus confidently. "You would kill me as soon as I turned my back. You are ruthless."

Now, he swung his leg into the struggling Abe, who weakly staggered backwards. Abe fell to the ground, losing the grip on his sword as he did so, before rolling onto his back.

Now, he looked up at Marcus.

"No wait!" Abe croaked, raising his arm feebly, as if to stop the blow. Marcus merely grunted in response, and then brought down the full weight of the war hammer down onto Abe's head.

He did not stop to look at what remained of his face...

As he looked around, it wasn't difficult to see the families now. Torches were placed around the top of the mound, and the families were stood in a circle around its center.

He walked silently up to them, grasping his war hammer. Many of them were armed. As he approached them, they parted, silently.

In the center of it all, was Mr. Tate, Aubrey, Preacher Harris and the witch, Elsie. Elsie gave him a crooked smile as he approached. It was Mr. Tate that spoke to him now.

"We will dispense with all the platitudes Marcus. You have come this far, and you deserve straight honesty." Mr. Tate said.

"That will be a refreshing change from you all," replied Marcus.

"If you love me, you will listen to him babe," said Aubrey.

"I will listen to him," Marcus replied.

At that moment, a horn resounded and was followed by a huge guttural roar. The sounds reverberated from the bottom of the mound. Immediately, Marcus saw the seven Bigfoots rushing up the mound, followed by Wes, Rusty and Ed.

None of the family members even flinched, in response to the attack. Rather, they stood in place silently, just watching the approach.

Now Marcus could see Hockran there, swinging a club, his face taught with rage.

Elsie shouted something now, and as she did so, a blue and obsidian light shot straight up into the air, pushing itself between Hockran and the families.

Marcus saw Hockran charge straight at the light, and then immediately bounce straight off it.

The other Bigfoots now joined him, and began pounding on the newly formed force field, but to no avail. Marcus could see that Ed was shouting something, but there was no sound at all now passing through the wall of light.

"As I was saying, before we were so rudely interrupted by our unexpected guests." said Mr. Tate.

"You expected them," said Marcus. "You planned this, I think."

"We did," said Mr. Tate. "We wanted all of our adversaries in one place. And now that we have them all together, it is time for the final test."

With that, he turned and nodded to Preacher Harris. Harris and two other men, then pushed four people, whose hands were tied behind their backs, to the front of the crowd, so Marcus could see them.

Marcus was surprised to see Giles, Marion, Emily and the girl from the mirror shop. They were all filthy and bedraggled. Giles in particular, looked like he had been beaten so badly, that he was almost unrecognizable.

"You see the final test is quite simple," said Mr. Tate. "You have to choose. You can choose to save one, of the three groups represented here . The Bigfoots, the shopkeepers, or your friend Ed and his two buddies. You can only save one group. The others will die. It's up to you."

"Why is that?" said Marcus. "Why would you have me make such an impossible choice? And how is there any benefit to you?"

"There is a benefit, my love," said Aubrey. "We have lived and prospered, for so many centuries now. We have a wonderful existence here, thanks to Elsie discovering the medicine."

"Our energy requires sacrifice though," said Aubrey, "It is not immortal. And, such a concentrated sacrifice as this, will give us enough strength to last for a thousand years."

"Don't you see, my love?" asked Aubrey. "Now, you can join us. Be my husband. We will have centuries to live together, and love together, in our beautiful world."

"This isn't a beautiful world Aubrey, it is evil! You kill with impunity to be what you are!" Yelled Marcus. "I don't think you even realize what you have become, or what is even driving you to be this way! I have an idea though."

Now, he reached into the sack. He pulled out the silver mirror, to which he had tied a turquoise stone. It was the same turquoise stone, given to him by the Clamash.

Now, he thrust the silver mirror, into Elsie's face. At first, she looked stunned. But, then she hissed, as she quickly transformed into her true self. She morphed into a hideous creature, all hunched over and twisted, with long pendulous breasts and tattered brown leathery wings.

She screamed at Marcus, while running straight towards him, her arms now transformed into nothing but twisted talons. As she was moving closer towards him, Marcus swung, the mirror around towards her.

The family members stood all around him. At that moment, they all began to sway, and started melting into nothing but dried husks, screaming as they did so.

Marcus swung his war hammer towards Elsie.

But, Elsie was suddenly being rushed by Katy!

Katy was surrounded by a brilliant, golden light. As she clashed full force into Elsie, they both shot straight up into the sky. Just a moment later, a mangled Elsie fell lifeless from the sky.

Far above Marcus, in the night sky, a star of shimmering, golden light still remained. Marcus caught his breath, expecting to see Katy reappear. But, the golden shimmer was all he could see.

It was at that moment, that Marcus felt a new peace and safety within his heart. He knew that Katy indeed, had come to help him...at precisely the right moment. Then, the light was gone.

Marcus now turned to see the four shop keepers, who were huddled together and hugging each other. They too, were being transformed, but unlike the screaming family members they had smiles on their faces. Marcus saw Giles mouth a `thank you` to him, just before he too, turned to dust.

"Traitorous fools!" Shouted Mr. Tate. "You refused to join us at the beginning, and you have been trapped as slaves as a result ever since! You now die as slaves! At least I had the pleasure of watching you die before me."

"That is typical of you," Mr. Tate said Marcus. "Enjoying what you consider to be the suffering of others, even as you too die. The choices they made though, mean that they are not afraid of death. For you though, it is a very different story."

Mr. Tate had no time to reply. Rather, he stared in anguish at Marcus for a moment, just before he melted away.

"Babe," stammered Aubrey. Marcus looked at the now decrepit figure of Aubrey. She was the last of the family members left. A huge strength of will seemed to be keeping her together, thought Marcus.

Evil In Ollenberry

He could see that she was gritting through her now rotting teeth as she spoke to him.

"Didn't you love me enough?" She said pleadingly. "Our life could have been so wonderful. Everything I did, I did for the family, for others. I wish you could have been with us. We had such a wonderful future together. She moved towards him with her arms outstretched, before arching her back, and shaking violently.

Then she was gone.

Marcus slumped to his knees. Suddenly the suit of armor felt heavy and hot, and he began furiously stripping it off.

Then he sobbed. He was still sobbing when the helicopters landed. Somebody was talking to him, but he refused to listen to what they were saying. All he wanted to do was to stay here.

Right in this moment...

CHAPTER NINE

-After Ollenberry-

"So, you do understand that you can never see Ed again, right?"

Marcus had been in this featureless building for days now. Maybe a week, if he had to guess. He wasn't sure though, because he had seen neither clocks, nor daylight in all that time.

The two men had been his constant companions during that time. One with blond hair, the other black. They were again dressed in immaculate grey suits, white shirts and black ties. They always wore sunglasses, even though he had only ever seen them indoors.

In the time he had known them, despite his questions, he had only learned one detail about them. Marcus only knew their names, which he doubted were genuine. They were Mr. Saunders and Mr. McGee.

"I understand that Mr. Saunders, I do." Marcus replied. "And, I also understand that I am to take on this new identity, and never speak to anyone about what happened in Ollenberry."

"Otherwise," said Marcus," I am to suffer what you called, unspecified serious consequences. You don't have to specify them though. I have no doubt, that they would be very unpleasant for me. I understand also, that you don't like to make these threats, but you have to. All of this is happening for the good of the nation. So you say."

"That's exactly right!" Mr. Saunders exclaimed. Then he said, "As you know, there was a large meteor that hit the earth, and destroyed the good folk of Ollenberry, just as they were having their festival on Dragon's Mound."

"Of course, it helps that not a trace of any of them were left," said Mr. Saunders. "It made the story much more plausible for the press to swallow, and much easier for us to clean up. No awkward autopsies, for example. I am sure you understand what I mean. Why, according to General Johnson, we should be even able to lift the quarantine zone a few weeks earlier than we planned."

"Then, the remaining inhabitants of Ollenberry can enjoy economic investments that they could have only dreamed of." said Saunders.

"I will have to admit, the Instagram video your former students posted, was tricky to deal with. It was not easy to explain video footage of a china doll, independently twisting her head around, paired with an audio recording of tortured screams."Mr. Saunders said, while shaking his head.

"Our techs were eventually able to pull it apart though." said Mr. Saunders. "They were able to persuade most of the viewers, that it that was nothing more than a fake. People would prefer not to believe in the truth, if it is disturbing, you see."

"Revolution in understanding, takes mental energy and determination. Better to avoid it if they possibly can, unless they are forced to do so." said Mr. Saunders.

"And what about the Bigfoots?" asked Marcus. "What will become of them?"

"Oh, we have already known about their existence for quite some time," said Mr. Saunders. "We have found scattered pockets of them in other remote areas. What truly remarkable creatures they are. Their leader, Hockran is a truly remarkable individual. Very intelligent, and so in tune with the natural world. Humans could learn a great deal from him, but he is extremely suspicious of us, and understandably so."

"Anyway, he has accepted relocation, with what remains of his clan. We have found an ideal location for them, many miles away from human habitation. I can assure you that he and his clan will be happy there." said Mr. Saunders.

Evil In Ollenberry

"As for you," said Mr. Saunders, "the witness protection program will take care of you now. Providing that you do what they say, you will be fine. We will finish up what we have left to do here."

"Your friend Wes is a slight risk," said Saunders. "He might stumble one day, after he has had a few drinks, even though he has been warned not to. The vast majority of people won't believe him though. After all, a meteor causing devastation is highly unusual, but not impossible."

"The very idea that an evil entity, could twist people to live hundreds of years, simply to feed off of the malevolent energy, is a ridiculous notion to most. He will go down as a crackpot conspiracy theorist if he does talk." said Saunders.

"And," said Mr. Saunders," We will be watching for that terrible creature. We will continue to watch, in case it did survive the battle with the benevolent entity. The one you call Katy. No evidence has been found of either of them, though."

With that, the two men rose from the table. "Enjoy your new life, Marcus," said Mr. Saunders. "It is a sweeter future than the deadly one you would have had."

...

Ed felt terrible. He had no idea where Marcus had gone, but he was assured by those two government men, that he would be okay. He knew that Marcus would never be able to contact him again, and although deeply saddened, he did understand why.

Still, in the weeks that followed, he was barely able to sleep. So, he didn't see the cloud following him as he turned down the quiet desert road...

...

Marcus enjoyed the beauty of The Great Smoky Mountains. Although he was lonely, he never doubted he had done the right thing. In trying to heal, he lost himself in hiking and exploring in the mountains.

Sometimes, when the air was still and he was high up on the ridges, he thought he could hear Aubrey whisper his name. She was just dust now though, swirling and dancing in the wind, he thought.

So, it couldn't be true...

Evil In Ollenberry

The End.

Printed in Great Britain
by Amazon

20768059R00149